LIGHTS AT MIDNIGHT
BOOK 1

Lights at Midnight

Copyright © 2020 by Orchid Leigh

All rights reserved

This is a work of fiction. Names, characters, businesses, places, events and incidents are either the products of the author's imagination or used in a fictitious manner. Any resemblance to actual persons, living or dead, or actual events is purely coincidental.

Printed in the United States of America

www.OrchidLeigh.com

LIGHTS AT MIDNIGHT
BOOK 1

ORCHID LEIGH

For my little mermaid Leila

1

You never expect it—and I guess that's for the best. It's not like you can ever prepare for it, because when your life changes from ordinary to extraordinary, it doesn't give you any warnings. It grabs hold like a riptide, fierce and strong, sweeping you up against your will and tossing you with the current. Sometimes you can do nothing but hold your breath and wait. It's scary. But with time, you find your strength again, and you can take that chance and swim.

It's hard to pinpoint the exact day my unexpected life began. I sometimes think it was the day we received the notice of inheritance from my grandmother. Or maybe it was the day we packed up and actually set off for Ocean Lake. Or perhaps it was the day I met . . .

No, I'll start my story with the move.

"Do you think we can fit it?"

"Seriously?" I wriggled my nose. "I really don't think we can fit any more, Dad."

"The other one's in there somewhere," he said, tilting a sorry head at me. "I need my shoe."

"I guess." I lifted my feet so Dad could throw his shoe in with the others already down there playing footsie with me.

"There we go," he said. "Oh, and Millie's blow-dryer." He pulled the plastic dryer from under his arm and reached across to wedge it somewhere near my elbow. "Okay, that should do it." He narrowed his eyes at me. "You gonna be okay in there?"

I squirmed in my seat, trying to get comfortable in the messy nest I'd made among all our stuff. We were only taking what we could cram into this small car, but it sure seemed like a lot. And it *was* a lot—it was everything. It was our whole lives, condensed and sorted, and shoved in the back of this old beater car with me.

I stared back at Dad, who was looking at me with concern. "Yeah," I said with my well-practiced smile. "I'm good."

"You sure?"

"Yeah, I'm fine. Thanks, Dad."

"Okay, Ellie," he said. "I guess it's time." He slammed the car door, but it caught and jammed on something. He pulled it back open and kicked at the boot that had gotten in the way.

He tried again. This time it stuck.

Dad moved to the driver's seat next to Millie and started the car.

I stared out my window and sighed. "Bye," I said to the only world I'd ever known. I drew a farewell heart on the steamy glass and watched the city fade from view as we rolled away.

We were heading to a new life, a new home tucked way up there in middle-of-nowhere Maine. It was so small and so hidden that when I searched for it online, I almost missed it, even with the bright red map marker hovering right over it. I had to zoom in for forever before seeing anything, and when I did spot the small dot of a town, I sat frowning at the computer screen for a good ten minutes, dismayed by what I saw or, more accurately, what I didn't see.

I had been sitting in the living room with my laptop, and I kept turning my head from the screen to the window that looked out over our busy street in Brooklyn, then back to the screen again in shock.

Oh boy. Life was about to get a whole . . . lot . . . simpler.

This move was on me, though. Yep. My fault. So I couldn't complain. I was the one who had inherited the house, after all. How could I blame Dad for wanting to take it? I couldn't.

I always knew Dad wasn't made for the city. He was from Texas and was a true country boy at heart if I ever saw one. When he came home from his stressful corporate job that day and picked up the letter from the counter, I watched with a heavy heart as his good news hit and brightened his weary face. It wasn't something I could just ignore.

My poor dad had been raising me alone since I was a baby. He and my mom moved to the city on a whim after they married, but it had been a dream of hers, and I always assumed he just went along with it to make her happy. She was a dancer who was working full time as a waitress when she got pregnant with me. She died from complications related to childbirth, and after that, I think Dad, secure in his job and with a new baby to raise, just stayed in the city, feeling stuck and alone.

Millie came along about a year ago. She and Dad met at an open mic night at his favorite honky-tonk bar in the East Village. She got up to sing a Dolly Parton song, and his big country heart fell pretty hard after that; they'd been inseparable since.

I liked Millie. She was a pretty, bubbly blonde woman who laughed and talked a lot. Her friendly Southern accent was easy to listen to, though, and she had a way of making Dad laugh. I liked her for that.

Millie dressed like she was always ready for a party or an evening out with flowery dresses and a face of pretty makeup that was perfectly applied any and every time I saw her. And she always smelled good: a sweet combination of perfume and hairspray and fragrant lotions that mixed well with her equally sweet personality.

She was ten years younger than Dad, who had just turned the ripe old age of fifty last year, and her bright, cheerful demeanor was a stark contrast to his more solemn mood. He seemed to like her, though, and I was always happy to see Dad smile more. And with Millie, we both did.

It was a cold day in the middle of February, just a few days after my fifteenth birthday, when we finally made the move. The time had come. School was on winter break, and Dad had just scored a "great deal" on this old clunker we now rattled down the road in.

I watched out the window as a messy mix of snow and rain fell from the gray sky above. Dad turned on the wipers and smeared the mess around the window, clearing as much as the tattered blades would allow. I did an equally sloppy job of pushing down my doubts.

I was keeping them to myself—at least I was trying to. I didn't really know what my problem was, and it wouldn't be fair to take this opportunity away from Dad without a good reason, right? Right. So I pushed them down and swallowed them. *Gulp.*

My arbitrary doubts didn't make much sense, anyway. No, I didn't want to leave my home and my friends, but there was more to it. Leaving New York made me sad, not nervous. And these doubts I was struggling with left me feeling apprehensive and a little scared, to be honest.

I couldn't quite pinpoint what it was, but my gut, the thing that was usually pretty reliable and trustworthy, was telling me this move was bigger than just a move—like it mattered more somehow. It was stupid, I knew, but the feeling was strange and unsettling, and I couldn't shake it.

The letter of inheritance came addressed to me, Cordelia Amora Heart. Yes, that's my full name. And yes, I know it's a bit of a gooey mouthful. Don't worry, most people just call me Ellie. Cordelia was my mother's name, though, so I hold a place for it. It just seems a little too regal for a normal girl like me.

When somebody uses my full name—in all its gooeyness—I know it's serious. And that letter came jam-packed with a lot of serious stuff.

The letter explained I had inherited a house in Maine from my great-grandmother on my mom's side. It was very much a surprise because my mom had been adopted as a baby, and Dad said not even she would have known of her biological grandmother from Maine. But somehow, this grandmother knew of me, and in her will, she had given her house and property of 15 Ivy Lane, Ocean Lake, Maine, to me.

"This is it," said Dad.

I perked up. I glanced out my window just to see the same

dense forest I'd been looking at for the past two hours. But apparently this stretch of forest rolling by was a more specific stretch of forest, and I saw a small sign welcoming us to Ocean Lake just as we rolled past it.

"There are other people in this town, right, Dad?" I asked, trying my best to joke about it, but man, was this depressing.

Dad's sympathetic eyes found mine in the rearview mirror. He turned down another road, but it proved to be just as disheartening as the one before it. "This must be town," he announced.

Yep. I recognized it from the photos I'd seen online, but without the zoom feature, it seemed so much smaller. It was cute. I guess I could give it that. And it had everything. Yes, it sure did, and I had to keep my eyes popped and wide so I wouldn't miss it. We rolled down Main Street, scrolling past the regular gas station and post office, a few mom-and-pop shops, an old diner, and a shabby-looking gazebo right in the center of it all. That was it—the tour was over.

Dad turned off the strip and onto a gravel road. We followed along the edge of a large frozen lake, and my disappointment in the lacking town was instantly made up for.

"Now how did I not see this?" I gasped, feeling short of breath because it had been taken by the view in front of me.

I thought back to my adventures on the online map and tried to remember. No. It hadn't been there, not in any of the photos and not in the aerial view from above; I would have seen it. It was too big to miss.

I was mesmerized. It was still early, but the winter sun was readying to set, and a cotton candy sky created a breathtaking backdrop set against the icy waters. I stared transfixed as the light shimmered and bounced off the ice crystals in a dreamy display.

The lake was mostly deserted, except for in the distance, someone was running along the rocky shore, a black dog trailing behind. We drove closer. It was a boy . . . about my age. He had a stick in his hand, getting ready to toss it . . .

"Okay, it should be coming up here on the left," mumbled Dad. He turned the wheel.

We slowly rolled onto another gravel road and continued into a thicket of trees. Around another bend was a rustic wooden fence outlining the front perimeter of the property.

It appeared as we climbed a steep hill. A large farmhouse with a long dirt driveway leading to a massive old barn. Everything was white, blending beautifully into the rolling, snowy hills behind it. The land behind the house stretched and sloped for some time before dissolving into a dense forest.

We pulled into the pebbled driveway and stopped. Dad turned around in his seat to face me.

"You ready for this?" he asked.

I shrugged, unsure.

2

We entered through a side porch and stepped into a spacious and, to my confusion, completely stocked and furnished kitchen.

"Oh my god, Dad. Is this right?" I turned to Dad and Millie to confirm we had entered the right house. I was afraid we were accidental intruders into somebody's well-loved and lived-in home. They both shared the same expression of shock I knew had surfaced on my own face.

Dad, with the house keys still in hand, glanced down to double-check the address on the printout he was holding. "Yep," he said, looking no more convinced.

"Wow," Millie and I uttered in unison. We were all still standing in shock at the door.

The kitchen was a busy mess of stuff and then more stuff. I examined the chaos with fascination. Colorful porcelain dish sets were stacked on open shelves.

A chandelier of copper and iron pots hung in the center above a hefty stone-topped island. Under a cabinet, mismatched mugs dangled from hooks. There were decorative knickknacks everywhere, and in a corner, a sizeable collection of worn and torn cookbooks accumulated on a cluttered baker's rack.

Tucked away to the side, in a little window nook, was a small table with a slender vase that held a single yellow rose. The vase was resting on top of a piece of notepaper. I walked over to it.

"Oh, my heavens, Jim," said a breathless Millie as she scanned the space. "Did you know it would be furnished?" She turned to Dad.

"Nope. They said the house and the lot were to go to Ellie, but no one mentioned a full-on country flea market," he said.

"It's fully stocked!" gasped Millie as she opened a pantry door. A plethora of boxes and cans filled and spilled from the shelves.

I looked closer at the paper on the table. It was a handwritten note. I picked it up and read it.

Welcome home, Cordelia.

All you'll find here is yours, and my hope is that you will love and cherish it as I did. This house was filled with love and was loved. May it bring to you the same joy it brought to me.

Please know it is not a gift, for it has always been yours. It belongs to you, just as it did to me. My soul could not bear to give it to another for fear it would fall into the wrong hands, so it remains yours to do with it what you will. And I worry not, for I know I am leaving it in the palms of someone very special and capable indeed.

Remember to follow your heart and let love guide you in all that you do, for it is where your strength and happiness lie.

Your loving,
Granny Leira

I picked up the letter and handed it to Dad.

"Isn't that something," he said, scanning it and passing it to Millie, who read it with a smile.

"It sounds like she was a lovely woman," said Millie. "It sure is a shame we never met her." Millie handed the letter back to me. "I think this will be the first thing that you'll want to cherish."

I took the letter and tucked it into my pocket.

"Now, come on," said Millie. She reached for my hand. "Let's go find our rooms!"

We entered a cozy living room, just as busy and stuffed as the kitchen before it. We turned the corner and climbed a staircase and found ourselves in a dark hallway with several closed doors. We opened one.

It was a large room with an oversized oak poster bed in the center. There was a picturesque bay window on one wall. On the opposite side, an opened door showcased a large bathroom glistening in white marble and chrome.

Just inside the bathroom, Millie turned a knob to reveal a large walk-in closet. She entered, mouth agape.

"Oh my!" she gasped. "Look at this!"

A euphoric smile spread across her face as she stared at the walls of empty racks and cubbies. She turned to me.

"This is a really nice room. What do you think?"

I scrunched up my nose. "Eh . . . It's okay," I said, unimpressed. The dark polished wood and the swirl motifs that decorated the bedposts and matching dresser were way too fancy.

"Do you mind if your dad and I take this one?" she asked.

"Oh yeah, definitely," I said, laughing at her. She was always too nice to me and this was obviously the master bedroom. "I'm gonna keep looking."

Millie let out a high-pitched squeal. She bounced over to me and squeezed me in a tight hug.

"Oh, thank you, thank you!" she said. "This room! Oh my goodness! I love it! Look at *this* closet! I have dreamt of a closet like this my whole life!" She pressed her hands to her cheeks joyously and twirled to admire her new room.

I laughed at her again and slowly made my way back out the door. "I'm gonna go look around."

"Okay, hon," she said, waving a happy hand at me.

There were a few more doors along the hallway. I found a bathroom, a couple of closets, and another small room, messy and piled high with more junk. It could work, but I didn't want to clean it, and I wanted to see what else the house might have to offer.

At the end of the hall, I reached the last door and opened it to a flight of stairs. The attic.

The room was quaint and lovely.

The white paneled walls and ceiling slanted low to create a

small, cozy den-like space, where a string of fairy lights sparkled and swooped in a scalloped pattern along the top edge.

At the far end of the room, a single window looked out to the back of the property, and on the ceiling above, a large skylight opened up to a gray winter sky.

The bed was an overstuffed mattress that lay unframed on the wooden floor. It had a colorful patchwork quilt with a multitude of pillows tossed casually on top.

I placed my backpack among the pillows and smiled. This felt right. I wasn't sure why. I scanned the quiet room, breathing a sigh of relief. I took my grandmother's note from my pocket and read it again. I reflected on the first line—the first thing she had ever said to me.

Welcome home, Cordelia.

I unpacked and sorted my things while Dad and Millie prepared dinner downstairs.

I pulled my journal from my backpack. I would need a place to hide it. It wasn't like Dad or Millie to go snooping in my stuff, but I always felt a little freer to write my secrets when I knew they would be hidden away.

My room had a small built-in cabinet near the top of the stairs. I opened it. The space inside was shallow, with the back slanted in line with the roof. I pulled the light on.

There were several shoe boxes stacked inside. I picked one up and opened it. It was filled to the brim with old photos.

Many of them were of a pretty woman with red hair so gorgeously bright I might have thought it was dyed. But I recognized this color.

I pulled on the streak of red tucked low on the back of my head. I had always had it, this strange burst of color among otherwise regular dull blonde hair. My mom had it, too—Dad said she did—and now I guess I knew where it came from.

These photos were of my grandmother. They were of her around the house: one of her reading in a chair in the living room, another of her in her garden, and several more of her with a young boy and a man who I thought must have been my great-grandfather.

Many of the photos were overexposed, being just a blurry mess of light, and I couldn't make out what they were of. There was one I thought might be an image of a horse, but I couldn't be sure.

I picked up another box. This one was very light. I didn't expect to find much in it at all. I opened it to reveal a red silk scarf.

I unfolded the fabric and found inside a golden, heart-shaped locket. There were swirly, ornate details etched in the gold, with an oversized heart-shaped diamond resting in the center.

Inside was another photo. I squinted and looked closer. If it hadn't been for the dark hair in this black-and-white photo, I might have thought this picture was of me. It was my grandmother again; I was sure. She was younger, though, probably just a few years older than I was. She looked happy. She smiled with her eyes and was as lovely as the locket itself.

I strung the locket around my neck and placed my journal in the box, securing it secretly among the others.

"How's the room, Ellie?" asked Dad. We were sitting down for dinner at an old farmhouse table in the dining room.

"Oh my god, I love it," I said, reaching for the bread in front of me and taking a joyous bite. I was so happy and relieved to ditch the pretense.

Dad raised a cheerful eyebrow to Millie. "Well, that's certainly good to hear," he said. "Your grandmother has gone out of her way to make us feel at home, hasn't she?"

With a mouthful of bread, I smiled at him.

"What's that?" asked Millie.

"Wha?" Breadcrumbs sprayed from my mouth.

"The chain around your neck." She pointed at me.

Realizing she meant the locket, I pulled it out from under my shirt. Millie's mouth dropped. They both stared in silence.

"What's wrong?" I asked.

"Can I see it?" Millie stretched out her hand.

I unhooked the clasp and handed it to her. She carefully turned over the locket, shining the overhead lights through the diamond. The light sparkled and danced.

"Jim, I think it's real," she said in stunned disbelief.

She handed it to Dad.

He turned it over the same way Millie had and let out a troubled cough.

"You say you found this upstairs in a shoebox?" he asked.

"Yeah," I said defensively. I didn't like the way they were looking at me. I was beginning to wish I had left it there. "The girl looks like me, so I thought I could have it." It was a weak line of reasoning, I knew.

Dad opened the locket. "How about that? She does. Just about your age, too." He closed it again, regarding me solemnly. "You're not going to be able to wear it, Ellie."

"But, Dad!" I protested.

"Hey, I'm not saying it's not yours, but you can't *wear* it. This locket looks old, and if that very large diamond is real—"

"I doubt it's real, Dad."

He inspected it again and swallowed audibly. "Probably not," he mumbled, more to himself than the room at large. "But if it is, it's worth a fortune." He paused on the diamond a second longer, then raised his eyes to mine. "You might lose it, Ellie. And if you don't, someone will steal it right off your neck."

I put my hands around my neck, imagining the horror. "Okay," I conceded. "So where do I keep it?"

"Certainly not in a shoebox!" scoffed Millie.

"No, certainly not," agreed Dad.

We all decided to put the locket in the safe where Dad kept his passport and other important items. I felt a little sad to part with it. To me, it didn't make any sense to hide something so lovely away. But it was two against one, and I knew they were probably right.

"This is one you can trust me on, Ellie," said Dad as I handed it over. "You'll thank me one day. I promise." He closed the safe and turned the key, and that was that.

For now.

4

I stood on our front porch and breathed in the remarkably fresh, fresh air, thinking now *this* was something they couldn't put on maps or in photos.

It was one of those unusually warm days right smack dab in the middle of February, sandwiched between the biting winter before and what was surely left of it.

I listened to the birds singing their happy symphony in the sun and smiled when, every once in a while, they'd fall perfectly in step with the beat the drippy gutters were providing.

The door opened behind me. Dad strolled past me on his way to the car, still busy unpacking our old life.

"Can I walk to town?" I asked.

Dad heaved and pulled out the last and largest suitcase. He plunked it on the ground. "Yeah, but take your phone."

"I got it," I said, skipping down the driveway.

On the street, I passed the lake, frosted in a blanket of ice and snow. It was deserted and quiet. And in the placid silence, I had a strange idea: that within the whistle of the warm wind blowing so pleasantly around me, the frozen water called out my name . . .

I was smiling when I turned off the long gravel road and onto Main Street.

The center of town was a busy beehive compared to the lake. The warm weather seemed to have lured out most of the small town's few inhabitants, and they jogged, strolled, and scurried past the shops in town.

I spotted the local store, Carle's Market, and headed over. A bell chimed when I entered the busy market, and many curious eyes crept my way.

In a rush to avoid the glares, I quickly turned down an aisle and smacked right into somebody. Our heads collided with a loud *thud* and I doubled back in pain.

"Oh my god!" I cried. "I'm so sorry!"

I glanced up to see a boy standing with his hand rubbing his forehead. I immediately recognized his rusty orange coat and shaggy brown hair. He was the same boy I had seen at the lake last night.

"Are you okay?" I asked, feeling like a clumsy fool.

He moved his hands to his pockets. "Yeah, I'm okay," he said quietly.

"God, my head's still pounding!" I was holding my forehead, waiting for the pain to subside. "Are you sure you're okay? You can tell me. Don't spare my feelings."

"I'll be all right," he said with a laugh. "What about you?" He was looking at my hand still on my head.

I lowered it. "Is it red?"

"Yeah, it is. A little. You all right?"

"Yeah," I said, rubbing my head again.

I then lowered my hand to peer more closely at the kid in front of me. With the subsiding pain, my vision was clearing. I straightened up and smiled a little sweeter at the cute boy staring back at me.

He had a nice smile, and his muddy, disheveled hair hid good eyes. And sprinkled just on the bridge of his nose was a cute scatter of dark freckles. I continued to smile and stare, but I didn't realize it until he glanced away uncomfortably.

I cleared my throat. "So where's your dog?" I asked.

He looked at me sideways. "My dog? How do you know—"

"I saw you last night by the lake," I said, cutting him off.

"Oh . . . uh . . . ya did? Sh-She's at home." He stumbled over his words awkwardly and his shy eyes darted back to the candy.

I smiled at him, finding his clumsy struggle amusing. "Yeah, we're new here. We just drove in last night."

"Yeah," he said. "I know."

"You know?"

"I figured," he corrected.

"Huh," I said, feeling the world around me close in a little. "This small-town stuff is weird."

He nodded in agreement. "Where are you from?"

"New York. Brooklyn."

"Geeez," he said in a long wheeze that flowed out until all his air was gone. "Why would you move here . . . from there?" He looked at me like I was crazy. Actually crazy.

"Eh . . . my dad," I said.

"Well, I'm sorry about that."

He was so serious that I laughed. "So what's your name?" I asked.

"Peter," he mumbled. He was back to being shy and shuffled his feet a little.

"I'm Ellie."

He smiled at me, then quickly went back to the candy.

"What are you going to get?" I asked.

"Um . . . not sure . . ."

"Twix are good," I suggested.

"Yeah, I like those, too," he said. He picked up a Twix pack and turned to me. "It was nice meeting you, Ellie."

"You too, Peter. Maybe I'll see you around sometime."

He nodded and rounded the corner to the register.

I sat and stared absentmindedly at the candy for another minute, still thinking of the dull ache in my head and the boy I had smashed it into.

"Hey, Ellie." I turned, surprised to see Peter again. He was reaching around the corner with his hand out to me. "Here," he said. It was a sample pack of Advil. "For your head." He put a bottle of water in my other hand. "Don't worry. Carle knows they're paid for."

He smiled at me, then disappeared around the corner again.

I sat at the gazebo alone—and feeling it, in this small town, so isolated and far from everything. The sun shining down helped some, and I was trying to soak in its bright mood as I sat in a sunny spot, people-watching and drinking the water Peter had bought for me.

Everybody else at least seemed like they were succeeding in their efforts to be happy. The warm day was receiving a warm welcome, and I watched as people flowed in and out of the stores, looking delighted to be rid of the burden of winter and the puffy coats that came with it—even if just for a day.

I was about to get up and head back home when I saw Peter again. He exited a small diner and stopped to hold the door for an elderly couple. He waited patiently with a big smile on his face as they toddled through, then waved them goodbye and turned down an alley and was out of sight.

A smile lingered on my face as I started toward home and down the road that opened up in front of the lake.

The icy water glistened beside me. The bright noon sun beamed on its brilliant white surface, creating a stunning spectacle of light so beautiful that my eyes were frozen to it. It begged and pleaded for my attention. I heeded its call and proceeded down the rocky embankment.

A pebbled beach ran along the edge of the water for some time before merging into the dense forest surrounding it. The winter trees, set against the icy waters, created a sight that was completely breathtaking, and I imagined I might find this exact image on a postcard if I were to go check in one of the local shops in town.

I walked down a long dock that stretched out on top of the frozen surface. I stopped at the edge and stared down at the dazzle of light that playfully danced and sparkled on the ice. I was hypnotized by the beauty and felt a sudden beckoning come over me, as if the water was calling my name again. I closed my eyes and imagined a warm day, the hot sun on my skin, the cool water below me, waiting for me, waiting to soothe, waiting to wash me in its coolness.

The feeling, the desire to jump in, was so strong. I opened my eyes before it could take over. I looked down again at the frozen water, but I still felt the pull to go in.

I shook my head to shake it off. "What the heck has gotten into me?" I asked aloud to the silence, but I stood still with my gaze transfixed on the frozen water in front of me.

"Got any plans today?" asked Dad. He was dressed in a suit and tie for his new job. His peppered hair was freshly cut and combed and sprayed into place.

Fancy-work-Dad was always so strange to me. Dad to me was a T-shirt and flannel, with a beer or guitar in his hand. That attire didn't cut it for most financial consultant positions, so he swallowed it, but I only ever saw him dressed so spiffy like this in the early mornings before work.

He was busy packing his lunch and coffee.

"I don't know. I might walk back down to the lake later. Is that okay?"

"Make sure you let Millie know." Dad zipped up his lunch pack, looking glum. "Well, back to the grind for me today."

"Do you ever think about changing careers, Dad?"

Dad glanced up, pondering. "This is kind of a change." He straightened his tie stiffly. "Smaller company, at least."

"No," I said. "Something more fitting. More you."

"Like what?"

"I don't know." I eyed him up and down, thinking. "I think farming would suit you."

Dad laughed. "Farming? Huh?" He smiled at me. "You think this city boy could be a farmer?"

"A farmer?" asked Millie as she came into the kitchen.

"Yeah." I smiled at her. "Don't you think it would suit him?"

"I could see that," said Millie. She put her arms around Dad, kissing him. "Those poor cows, though." She laughed. "You do remember the fish, right?"

"Yeah." I laughed, remembering our poor fish, Larry. He hadn't lasted more than a day with Dad when Millie and I were away on a girl's weekend together. "Fish are hard, though," I said with mock empathy toward Dad.

Dad glared at me from under hard brows. "Let's just see how this new job goes before we start talking about a career change, aye? Maybe we'll be able to save some cows." He grinned and picked up his lunch and coffee.

"Good luck, Dad."

"Okay, baby," said Dad, kissing me on the cheek. "Have fun, girls." He kissed Millie goodbye and turned toward the door.

"Bye, Dad."

"Bye, babe," said Millie. She then turned to the kitchen. "I suppose I should finish unpacking and organizing all this stuff." She sighed. "It sure is a lot of stuff, huh?"

I surveyed the cluttered kitchen with her. "Yeah. Do you need help?"

"No, no," she said, still eyeing the room with apprehension. "This place is going to need all of my undivided attention." She turned to me, looking worried that maybe she had hurt my feelings. "If you don't mind."

"Oh no," I said quickly, happy to get out of it. The offer had been completely out of politeness, to be sure.

I spent the morning at my desk, doodling in my journal, then decided the ray of sun beaming across my hand from my window was a sign I should probably get out of the house.

I showered and got dressed, then tossed my journal into my backpack. I zipped it up and headed downstairs.

"Hey," I called to Millie as I filled a bottle at the sink. "I'm going to go out for a bit." I was having to shout over some pretty loud country music blaring from her cell phone. She was standing on a stool in front of an empty cabinet, dressed in jeans and a T-shirt, her tight-ringed curls pinned behind a red bandana. The counter below her was a clutter of teetering saucers and cups.

"Okay, hon," she said over her shoulder as she examined a couple of plates. She turned to me. "Oh, hey, can you mail those bills for me?" She pointed the plate she was holding at a stack of bills.

"Sure." I grabbed the pile of envelopes from the counter and swung the back door open.

It was another welcomed, warm day. Everything was melting and wet. I removed my coat before I even made my way down the driveway.

I walked down the road past the lake. It was still trying to entice me with its beauty, but I decided I would come back to it after I mailed the letters.

I found the post-office at the other end of Main Street, past Carle's Market and just a short swim past the gazebo. I quickly made it there and shoved Millie's stack of bills into the mail slot I located in the post office lobby.

I started to feel excited about the idea of going down to the lake and headed back in that direction.

I turned onto the sidewalk and saw, down the street ahead of me, a shaggy-haired boy with an orange coat—it was Peter again. He turned into Carle's Market. I picked up my pace, hoping to reach the store before he left.

As I approached, a group of three boys wearing matching red basketball jerseys shuffled out of the back of a black SUV. They entered the store ahead of me. I moved toward the store to go in but stopped with my hand on the door, peering inside through the window.

Peter was in the checkout line. The boys who had entered before me had stopped to talk to him, but he stood rigid with his eyes on the floor and he didn't seem to be having too much fun.

"Hey, look who it is, Boozer Jr.," one boy called to his friends. The boy who was a good foot taller than Peter reached over and ruffled Peter's hair. He tried to pull away, but the kid kept pestering him, while the other two boys just stood around and laughed. Peter did his best to ignore them and moved up the line to pay for his bag of chips.

The cashier gave the bully kid a stern eye, and the group turned its attention to the slushie machine.

Peter paid and shuffled toward the exit with his head still down. I hurried out of sight and ducked around the corner alley. I didn't want him to see me staring at him like this.

I waited a few minutes, then stepped back out. I glanced

down the street in both directions, searching for Peter. He was gone. I sighed, knowing I'd missed my chance to try hanging out with him.

I went back to Carle's to check there. The other boys were buckling back into their car with their mixed slushies in hand. The car door was still open, and one of the laughing kids smiled at me when I passed by. I glared at him and sent a mean thought missile in his direction before turning into the store.

Peter wasn't in Carle's. I grabbed some snacks from the store and started toward the lake, feeling depressed and alone. But the thought of the lake soon had me skipping, and when I turned down the road in front of it, I smiled.

Peter had made it there ahead of me. He was sitting at the end of the dock, eating his bag of chips. I walked over to him, passing his abandoned coat on the beach, and threw mine on top of it. I guess I was being too quiet because he didn't notice me as I approached. He was lost in thought and looked miserable for it.

"Hey, Peter," I called a little too loudly. He jumped in his seat, staring up at me without a word. "I'm not bothering you, am I?"

He scrambled to his feet. "Oh, no. I was just leaving." He started to go.

"No, wait," I said. "Can't you hang out?"

He turned back and narrowed his gaze, looking confused and unsure. "You want to hang out with me?" he asked, like the question didn't make any sense to him.

"Yes, pleeease," I begged, drawing out my plea in a long sigh that made me sound lonely and pathetic—but I was.

His narrow eyes held tight to their uncertainty.

"Come on," I tried again. "I got candy." I brought my backpack up in front of me and propped it in my arms.

Peter glanced around again. "Yeah, okay. I guess," he said with a shrug, but I thought he seemed happier than he was letting on.

"Good," I said happily. I moved to the edge of the dock and sat down. I patted the space beside me, motioning for Peter to sit. He hesitated for a second, then followed.

I had spent the rest of my birthday money at Carle's, and I poured a pile of too much candy between us.

"Help yourself," I said. I pulled a Twizzler out of the pack and started to chew. Peter was quiet beside me. He seemed anxious and fiddled with his hands. I could tell by the way he was side-eyeing the candy that he wanted to have some. He was just being polite or shy about it or something.

"What do you like?" I asked, smacking my Twizzler filled mouth noisily at him. He shrugged. I placed my hand on top of a bag of Skittles. "Hmm?" I questioned, holding my head at a tilt while I waited for his answer.

"Sure," he said.

I picked up the Skittles. "Give me your hand."

Peter put out his hand to me. I held it in place while I poured too many Skittles out into it. The small pieces spilled and pinged quietly as they hit the dock.

"Oops." I laughed. "The birds can have those, I guess."

"Thanks," he said, closing his hand around as many as he could.

I smiled at him, then turned back to the water. "So how long have you lived here in Ocean Lake?"

Peter sighed. "My whole life," he said, sounding exhausted by it.

"And how long would that be?"

"Fifteen years," he said, popping a Skittle into his mouth.

"Me too," I said. "My birthday was just last week."

"Happy birthday," said Peter.

"How come you don't like it here?" I asked.

"I never said that."

"You didn't have to."

Peter shrugged, looking uncomfortable. He stared at his handful of Skittles, obviously not wanting to talk about it.

I eyed him, trying to think if I should pester or change the subject.

I glanced at the lake and then back at Peter again. "Hey," I said, leaning into him and reaching for one of his candies. "Five bucks I make it past that big crack in the ice." I pointed him toward a large crack in the middle of the lake.

"Okay," he said with a smile.

I took my Skittle and geared up to toss it. I looked over my shoulder at Peter. "Are you sure?" I asked. "You know, I used to play softball."

"You're on," he said, smiling at me.

I loaded my arm and threw. The Skittle sailed through the air and landed just an inch or two past my target.

"Yes! Ha!" I screamed. I reached my arms up and held them high, reveling in my victory. I lowered them and turned to Peter with a sneer. "Someone owes me five bucks."

"All right," he said, laughing. "How about double or nothing? If I make it past that second crack, then we're even."

He was pointing to a crack much farther than mine, and it was highly doubtful he would make it.

"Okay," I said, unfazed. "Go for it." I nodded toward the ice.

He stood up.

"Hey, you're cheating!"

"We never said." He shrugged and smiled at me slyly. He hurled his candy through the air. It flung from his hand impressively but fell short by half a foot.

"Oh, yeah!" I screamed. I got to my feet and punched a happy fist into the air. "You owe me ten bucks!" I shouted in Peter's face.

He laughed, reaching into his pocket for the money.

"Oh, no," I said, putting my hand on his arm to stop him. "I'm just playing. You don't really have to pay me."

"You sure?"

"Yeah," I said with a gentle punch to his shoulder. "I'm not going to bankrupt my new friend."

"Your friend?" he asked, sounding surprised.

"Yeah." I nodded at him. "If you want?"

He smiled but seemed hesitant. "Well, ten bucks wouldn't bankrupt me," he said, sitting back down on the dock.

"Oh yeah?" I asked, finding my seat beside him. "Where are you getting so much money?"

"Shoveling, mostly."

"Well, keep your money," I said. I had yet to work for any money in my life and was suddenly feeling guilty—and very lazy, for that matter. "It sounds like you earn it."

"Okay," said Peter. "I'll just buy you something with it later."

"Oh, no . . ." I started to protest, but he was already shaking his head at me.

I conceded with a smile and fixed my eyes on his cute freckles.

"What?" He wiped at a spot on his nose, thinking I had seen something.

"Oh, nothing," I said, not realizing I had been staring.

"You sure?" He was still wiping at his nose.

"Yeah," I said with a chuckle to myself. "You're good."

I peered at the lake, still smiling. I turned back to Peter, who was being quiet again. He was looking pensive and somber and thoroughly defeated.

"Do you like music?" I asked, reaching for my backpack.

He turned to me. "Who doesn't like music?"

"Here." I handed him an earbud. "Snow Patrol . . . good for the melancholy blues," I said with a sympathetic smile.

Peter smiled back weakly. "Why are you melancholy? Because of the move?"

"Yeah, I was," I said, "but I'm starting to think it won't be so bad."

Peter held the earbud to his ear. "'Chasing Cars'?" he requested.

"Sure," I said, pushing play on the song I already had open.

I leaned back, pulling the attached Peter with me. We lay on the dock and stared at the clouds. I closed my eyes and got lost in the music for a while.

I opened them again and looked over at Peter. His eyes were closed and there was a small tear drawing a line at the corner. He turned his head toward me and met my gaze. The song was still playing, and we stared at each other quietly while it drifted through our ears.

I pulled the earbud from my ear and let the music linger quietly in the background. "What's your last name, Peter?" I asked.

"Evans," he answered.

"You have good eyes, Peter Evans," I said, staring at him.

Peter pulled his earbud out and brought a finger up to wipe the tear. "Good eyes?" he asked, his voice husky and weak.

"Yeah, good. Like, I can tell you're a good person just by looking at them. Has anybody ever told you that?"

He laughed. "No. No one's ever told me that." He paused for a second, staring back. "You've got good eyes too. They're big and stormy, like the ocean."

My heart skipped a strange beat when he said "ocean." I tried to hang on to the odd feeling, but it faded like a dream.

I sighed and stared back at Peter. His good eyes on me were glazed and lost somewhere cold. "So why are you melancholy?" I asked.

He turned back to the clouds. "Because you played 'Chasing Cars,'" he said with a smile.

I laughed. "Yeah, maybe it didn't help like I thought it would. Sorry."

"It's okay," said Peter. "It's nothing . . . Just life, ya know?"

"Do you want to talk about it?"

He shook his head against the dock. "Not really."

"Okay," I said, getting back up and crossing my legs in front of me. "Then we won't." I reached for my bag and pulled out the water. "Here." I handed it to Peter.

He sat up and drank. "Thanks," he said, handing it back to me.

I took a sip, then returned the bottle to my backpack. I must have bungled the job of screwing the cap back on and water poured everywhere.

"Agh!" I cried.

"What's up?" asked Peter.

"My journal." I pulled it from my bag and held it up. I grimaced at its soggy state. I waited for it to stop dripping, then placed it in my lap to examine the pages.

"Is it okay?"

"Yeah. Not too bad. It's not really important, anyway. Mostly drawings and stuff."

"Can I see?"

I hesitated for a second, then moved closer to him. "Um . . . try not to read my ramblings, if you can," I said with a tentative smile.

Most of my drawings were centered on the pages with my scribbled thoughts and daydreams surrounding them. I carefully pulled the sodden pages apart, trying to find one without much writing. I landed on a drawing that filled up most of the space.

"Oh, wow. Dragons," muttered Peter.

"Yeah," I said, smiling. "I really like dragons. The scales and wings are fun to draw."

"You're really good." He stared down at my drawing, admiring it with a look of disbelief. "Look at the detail on those wings—that's incredible. I could never do anything like this," he said with his eyes still fixed on the page.

"Do you like to draw?"

He sat back up. "Yeah. Well, kind of. I make comic books. They're nothing like this, though."

"You'll have to show me someday."

"Yeah, maybe," said Peter. He frowned at my journal. "I'm sorry it got ruined."

"It'll dry," I said, unbothered by it. "I think it's time to start a new one, anyway." I looked at Peter, feeling happy. I thought I might be staring again and turned my eyes to the lake. "Maybe I'll come back here and draw this. It's so pretty."

"Yeah," agreed Peter. "It's a good spot."

"Why's it so secluded, though?" I asked. "Like, why aren't there any houses or people anywhere? It's weird nobody's here ice skating or fishing or anything. Doesn't it seem strange to you?"

"Yeah, well, I'm used to it," said Peter. "Nobody ever comes here. That's why I like it."

"Hmm . . ." I said, still lingering on the strangeness of this place. I gazed at the icy water in front of me and felt the urge for it again. "I'm sorry to tell you, but you just might have to share this lake with me."

"I'm okay with that," he said.

"Yeah?" I asked with a smile.

He nodded.

"It must be pretty here in the summer. I wish we could go swimming now."

"You like to swim?"

"Not usually this much," I said with a growing hunger in my voice, and I faded in a strange thought with the water somewhere.

"It is," said Peter.

"What?"

"Really pretty in the summer."

"Does it get crowded then?"

"No, never," said Peter. "It'll be all yours."

"Ours," I reminded him.

He smiled weakly and looked away.

I stared at his messy hair, feeling a little confused by his oscillating signals. "Why are you so leery about being friends with me?"

Peter shifted uncomfortably. "Ah . . . I'm sorry. It's not you. Trust me."

"Then what?"

He swayed his head, throwing his struggled thoughts around. He sighed. "Ellie, you don't want to be friends with me."

"Isn't it obvious I do?"

"Yeah, but I don't know why. And . . ."

"And what?"

He sighed and fiddled with a pebble caught between the doc boards. "Look," he said, "I just don't think I'm good for you."

I stared at him, thinking he was being really daft. "You know I can decide that for myself, right?"

"Yeah, but . . ." Peter shrugged and was quiet. I waited for him to go on, but he remained silent. I nudged his elbow with mine, trying to coax it out of him.

He sighed and threw the loosened pebble onto the lake. It dinged and bounced on the ice before stopping.

"I don't know," he said finally. "It's a small town, Ellie, and it's hard to get unstuck once you get a peg in you. I don't want to do that to you."

"You think hanging out with you is going to mar my reputation here?"

"It will," he said.

"Why? What did you do?"

"I didn't do anything," said Peter with an exasperated sigh. "It's my dad. He's the drunk. He's the one that ran out and left us with no money, no nothing. But it doesn't matter here. If your dad's a loser, then you're a loser." He shrugged. "And that's what I am to everybody. That's what everyone thinks, especially the kids here. They don't even talk to me." He threw another pebble at the lake. "You'd just be better off without me. Trust me."

I stared at him quietly for a minute, shaking my head the whole time. "Get up," I said finally.

He stared at me, startled. "What?"

"Get up," I repeated. I got to my feet and stretched out a hand to him. He grabbed it, looking unsure. I pulled him up to stand beside me, then walked down the dock a little, motioning for him to follow.

"Here," I said. I stopped and put my hands on his shoulders to straighten him out so the dock was directly behind him. I then reached for his hands and pulled them up across his chest. "Okay, stand like that." I left Peter with his hands crossed at his chest, then moved around to stand behind him. "Okay," I called out. "This is a trust exercise. I'm going to catch you."

Peter twisted and glanced over his shoulder apprehensively. "You want me to fall back?" I nodded at him. "How do I know I can trust you?"

"You know," I said. "You already know. Don't do it if you're not sure."

Peter turned, facing forward again. He took a moment and paused. His shoulders relaxed. They moved up and down with a steadying breath. Then, without hesitation, he fell straight back into my arms. I bent at the knees a little to counter his weight, but my hold on him was steady and strong.

"See," I whispered in his ear, still holding onto him. "You can trust me." He got up and turned to face me, staring at me blankly. "I don't care about any of that stuff. You can't ruin a reputation I don't care about. They can think what they think."

"Yeah?"

"Yeah, they're wrong anyway," I said. "A bunch of wrong meanies from the sound of it."

He laughed at that. "How do you know they're wrong? You don't even know me."

"I've got those good eyes," I said, tapping at my temples. "But I don't need them because it's easy to see."

Peter took a step toward me. "Are you for real?" he asked with disbelieving eyes.

"Um . . . I'm not sure what you mean."

"I mean, you really are moving here, and you really want to be friends with me? And you're really as nice as all this?"

I tilted my head with a smile. "Yeah," I said. "Really real." I pinched some skin on my arm to prove it.

"I think I'm supposed to pinch myself," Peter said with a laugh.

I brought up my arm and punched him gently on the shoulder. "There. Does that help?"

"I don't know." He shook his head. "It's just you're not what you'd usually expect on a normal day in Ocean Lake. You're like an angel or something . . . I feel like I could just kiss you," he blurted out. "Sorry, I just mean . . . um . . . that . . . um . . ."

I laughed as Peter struggled out of his mess of words. He grinned sheepishly.

I put a finger to my cheek. "Go ahead," I said. He laughed and leaned in and kissed the spot.

"See, I'm real." I smiled and twirled on my heels.

I stopped to face Peter again. He shook his head and wore a dumbfounded smile that stretched across his face. Without a word, he walked back to the end of the dock and picked up my backpack and candy. He slung the bag over his shoulder.

"Come on," he said, pulling on my arm. "I want to show you something."

6

"Where are we going?"

"I want to show you the trails."

"The trails?"

Peter was pointing down the beach to a densely wooded area.

"I should check in with my um . . . well, my Millie first. She's probably expecting me back soon."

"That'd be okay," he said. "The main trail wraps around and exits in your yard."

"My yard? How do you know where I live?"

"Oh," said Peter, reaching down to grab our coats. He handed me mine with a guilty grimace. "Um . . . you guys moved into Granny Leira's place, right?"

"Yeah," I said, still confused. "How did you know?"

"Small town," explained Peter with a sorry shrug. "Everybody here knows everybody. And everybody here knows everything about them. Sorry."

"Small town indeed." I laughed. This would take some getting used to. "So you knew I was coming?"

"Oh, no," said Peter. "It's not as bad as that. I just knew someone was."

"Did you know Granny Leira?"

"Yeah, I knew her," he said with a smile.

An unexpected bubble of jealousy floated up and popped at my heart.

"I used to work for her," explained Peter, "around the house. Mowing and stuff. She was a really sweet lady. A little eccentric, but sweet. She let me work anytime I wanted to and paid good. And she liked to cook and gave most of it to me and my family. She was always doing nice stuff like that. She even made my brother a baby blanket when he was born." Peter glanced at me curiously. "Was she your grandmother?"

"My great-grandmother. But I didn't know her. My mom was adopted, so I never met her biological family."

"That explains why I've never seen you visit," he said. "How'd you get the house then?"

"She gave it to me. In her will."

"You got this from her, too," said Peter. He tucked his hand behind my neck and gently pulled on the red tendril that sometimes peeked out.

I glanced at the bright color that shone so much brighter in the afternoon sun. I smiled at Peter. "You're the first person who didn't just assume I dyed it."

"It's the same exact color as Granny Leira's hair, and she didn't dye it. And I think she was well over a hundred when she died, too. Bright red hair—all the way to the end."

"Hmm . . . long life," I said, contemplating the nice

redheaded grandmother who was just a stranger to me. "So she was nice?"

"Yeah, she really was. A lot like you." He stopped walking and studied me for a second. He smiled and I could see something amusing in his eyes, but I couldn't quite read what he was thinking. He blushed a little and started walking again.

"What?" I asked, chasing after him.

Peter pulled his shoulders in and looked at me with narrowed, thinking eyes. "I can't say it," he said, shaking his head.

"You can't say what?" I asked, confused and now way more curious.

He smiled. "Don't make me say it."

I laughed. "You know, this is making me more curious and you could have said anything instead of this."

"I'm not a good liar," he said.

"Can you give me a hint?"

His smile stretched big and wide. "It's cheesy."

"How bad?"

"Pretty bad," he said, laughing.

"Just tell me. I won't judge."

"I'll tell you later."

"If you can tell me later, you can tell me now."

"No, you can still back out of being my friend right now. I'll wait till you're more attached."

"Okay, fine," I said, backing off. "But if you're going to make me wait, it better be super gooey. None of that sprinkled-on parmesan stuff."

Peter laughed. "I promise not to disappoint." He stretched out his hand. "After you," he said.

I stepped onto the trail, and my mouth fell open.

I had been expecting a tiny, overgrown path in which I would be swatting at branches and tripping over roots and rocks the whole way. What lay before us was a narrow road that twisted and curved, winding its way through the forest.

The trees formed an arched canopy over the wide path, allowing just a light dusting of snow cover, so even in the midst of winter, the forest floor was relatively clear. The bright sun filtered through the branches with only a few select rays reaching the ground and casting a glow of magical, scattered light.

"Wow," I said in a hushed whisper the forest seemed to command.

Peter was smiling at me. "It's great, huh?" he said. He started down the path.

"Who does all this?" I asked, scurrying after him.

He shrugged.

"You don't know?"

"No, I have no idea. It's always been like this, and the paths go for miles. And it's like the lake—no one else ever comes."

"Hmm . . . so beautiful . . ." I was craning my neck to view the canopy above. I glanced back down, feeling a little swoony. "Kind of hypnotizing, isn't it?" I swayed and bumped into Peter's shoulder.

"You okay?" he asked.

I turned to him with a smile. "Yeah. This is absolutely beautiful."

Peter nodded. "Can I show you something else?"

We turned down another path, walking until we came to a

clearing. It was a large, perfectly circular cutout in the trees, and it looked like a house-sized UFO had landed and cleared itself a spot in the forest. A blanket of snow, untouched, covered the ground.

"It's grass," said Peter. "In the summer. And wildflowers."

I stepped into the opening until I was centered in the large circle. I turned my feet on the snowy ground and stared up at the disc-shaped opening above.

"Huh," I said. "This wasn't on the map, either."

"The map?"

"Yeah, this isn't on the map online," I said. "I mean, we can't be that far from my house, right?"

"No, your house is just over there," said Peter, pointing at the trees.

"I would have seen it. I'm pretty sure." I paused, now doubting myself. "I definitely would have seen the lake, though."

"The lake?"

"It's not on the map, either. Haven't you ever noticed?"

"No, I guess I haven't."

I looked back at Peter. "It's pretty great," I said. "Thanks for showing it to me."

He nodded. "Thanks for coming with me. It's not as nice when you have no one to share it with."

"So you've never had a picnic here with anybody?"

He laughed. "A picnic? No, I've never had a picnic anywhere. Do people still do picnics?"

"Yeah, they do. And I want to come back in the summer and have one, okay?"

"Sure," he said with a grin.

I dreamed about that idea for a second, then got excited about a new thought. "Oh, and a campout!" I screeched, grabbing onto his arm. "Wouldn't that be fun?"

Peter laughed again. "Don't you have parents?"

"Eh . . . yeah," I sulked, knowing he was right. Dad wouldn't let me camp here.

"When we're older," said Peter.

I nodded at him. "Sounds like a plan."

The squish of our footsteps on the muddy forest floor and the sweet songs of the birds as they enjoyed their bath in the sunbeams added to the magic of this forest that had completely enchanted me. My mind wandered dreamingly to a far-off place somewhere with the lake, with my sweet grandmother, whom I never knew, and with Peter, who seemed to fit in so perfectly with whatever this new life of mine was.

"Your house is just up here," said Peter, pulling me from my daze.

I turned to follow in the direction he was pointing, but in my usual turn of clumsy unluckiness, my foot caught and twisted on an otherwise innocuous snow-covered divot.

"Ouch!"

A sharp stab pierced my ankle. I tipped away from the pain and Peter caught me by my elbow.

"You okay?"

"Yeah. It's my ankle. But I think it's okay. Stupid clumsy me like always."

"Can you walk?"

I tried to get up, but the pain shot through my foot again. "Ouch. Ouch. Ouch!"

"Okay. No, don't try that again. If you can lean on me for support, your house isn't too much farther. Or should I go get help? Is your mom or dad home?"

"Just Dad . . . and Millie." I winced. "But no, it's okay. I think I can manage." I braced myself using Peter's shoulder and pushed myself up. We took a couple of steps together. "This is okay. It doesn't hurt."

"Okay. Just through here, and we'll come up to the back of your house, near the barn."

I wobbled alongside Peter and we exited the forest and entered my backyard. We were on the side of the barn and in plain view of the kitchen window that looked out to the rear of the property. The door opened. It was Dad.

"Crap. My dad's home," I mumbled under my breath.

"Ellie?" called Dad. He quickly started toward us.

"Yeah, Dad. It's me," I called back. "Don't worry, I'm okay!" I was hoping to put him at ease before he reached us.

He crossed the distance between us quickly and was by my side, taking over as my walking stick, pushing Peter aside and doing an impressive job of completely ignoring him.

"What happened?" asked Dad.

"Oh, I think it's fine. I wasn't paying attention. I think it's just twisted."

He moved me to the house and plopped me down on the wooden porch swing.

Peter stood stiffly at the bottom of the stairs while Dad examined my ankle.

"Hey, Dad," I said, trying to get him to focus his attention on me and not my expanding foot. I was staring at Peter, who seemed nervous and unsure of what to do with himself. I wanted to introduce them so he didn't have to stand there like an awkward outcast.

"What were you doing in the woods? Millie said you were at the lake," Dad asked, ignoring me.

"Yeah, I was. I'm sorry. We just decided to come back through the woods since the trails lead here."

"I think it's just a sprain. I'll go get some ice." He got up and started for the door.

"Hey, Dad!" I called out again, trying to stop him.

"Yup?" he said, finally snapping out of his worried-dad mode.

I gestured to Peter. "Dad, this is Peter. He's a friend I met in town." Dad turned toward Peter. "Peter worked for Granny Leira here mowing the lawn and stuff," I added, thinking Dad might need a positive spin for this boy who brought me home limping.

"Is that right?" asked Dad.

"Yes, sir," said Peter, glancing up politely before his gaze reverted to his sneakers.

Dad eyed him for a minute, then turned to me. I screwed my face awkwardly—silently pleading—in an attempt to get Dad to be nice to him. His placid expression gave no signs I was getting through. He turned back to Peter.

"Well, Peter," he said. "Maybe we can find you some work around here come spring." His tone was kind and unassuming. I smiled at Dad—beaming and proud.

Peter's shoulders fell with relief. "Yeah, I could do that, sir."

"All right, we'll talk about it later." Dad opened the door. "Right now, I'm going to go get some ice for your foot," he said and went in.

"Hey, I should probably get going," said Peter. He climbed the steps and sat beside me.

"Oh, okay. Are you sure? You don't have to. My dad's fine. He was just worried about me."

"Yeah, I know. He seems cool. I should go, though. My mom's probably waiting for me. She usually needs me to babysit my brother when she works at night."

"Okay. If you have to. Hey, give me your phone so I can add my number."

I put out a hand.

"I don't have a cell phone," said Peter.

"Oh." I was perplexed. "Email then?"

"No, sorry. My mom's weird about the computer," he said, sounding embarrassed. "How about I just call you from my house?"

"Okay." I smiled. "We'll be old school."

"Do you have a pen?"

"Oh, yeah, check my bag. The front pocket."

He rummaged through the bag and found a pen. "What's your number?" he asked.

I grabbed the pen and pulled his hand into mine. I wrote my number on his palm and closed it.

"It was nice meeting you, Peter Evans," I said with a smile.

"You too, Ellie . . ." He fished for my last name.

"Heart."

"Ellie Heart," he said, bobbing his head and looking at me like he was stumped on something. "You're pretty cool, Ellie. And I'm still not sure if you're real."

I reached up and pinched his arm. "You think I'm cool, do you?"

"Yeah, I do," he said, laughing and rubbing my pinch away.

"You don't know me well enough if you think that. I can be quite a dork sometimes. Just wait, you'll see."

He laughed again. "Can't wait," he said, getting up and starting toward the driveway. "Take care of that ankle."

"Bye, Peter." I waved goodbye and watched as he headed down the road and out of sight.

My ankle ended up being a bigger pain in the butt than was necessary. The hole I tripped in wasn't even a hole; it was more like Bigfoot's thumbprint, really, but here I was with a big fat brace strapped to my foot, weighing me down and making me miserable.

I had been cooped up in the house for days now. Winter had come on fierce again. After that last warm day with Peter, an unrelenting cold front swooped in and hovered over our area like a ghost, frosty and mean. Now, a winter storm warning was in effect for our county, and we were hunkered down for the night with no prospect of leaving.

I hadn't heard from Peter since he left four days ago. I was beginning to wonder if everything was okay, but I figured he was just busy with his family. I had been primed my whole life to rely on cell phones, so it was hard to get past the idea that I couldn't text or call him, and the lack of communication was making me feel like I had been whisked away and plopped right back down into the Dark Ages.

I was upstairs, sketching in my new journal. It wasn't a drawing of Peter, but I *had* doodled his name in bubble letters a couple of times on Monday after our day together. Right now, I was staring out the window at the backyard, sketching the forest skyline. The jagged silhouette reminded me of the big buildings in the city, and I imagined I was back home, gazing out over the harbor.

I didn't miss it like I thought I would, but I tucked the fond memories of my other life somewhere warm and cozy in the back of my mind with a smile.

I continued to watch out the window. It was twilight—that lovely time of day just after the sun falls behind the horizon. It would be dark soon. But for now, the light lingered and lit the snowflakes as they began to slowly fall, one by one.

From up here, I could see the entire backyard. And beyond the forest, where the light was the brightest, I could just make out the dark and distant lake.

I imagined on a sunny day it would be glistening and sparkling in the sunlight. And I longed for a hot summer day where Peter and I could swim and play by the dock until nightfall. I wondered again where he was.

There was quite a commotion coming from downstairs. Dad and Millie were enjoying their respite from adulthood, and it sounded as though Millie had had one too many glasses of wine. Dad had his guitar out and they were singing and playing their favorite country tunes together. Millie's high-pitched laughter played easily over the music, and to my surprise, there was an occasional note of laughter from Dad. It was a side of him only Millie could bring out, and it always made me love her that much more.

The sky had darkened now, and my drawing was either finished or would have to be completed another day. It didn't matter. I closed my journal and turned to check my phone again. Maybe I had missed a call from Peter—no.

That was when I saw it: a quick, bright flash of light coming from outside. *What was that?* I turned back to the window, but all was black. I got up to flick the light switch on the wall, then pressed my nose to the windowpane.

I strained my eyes but saw nothing. It could have been lightning, I told myself. *Thundersnow,* I remembered from science class. Surely, that was all it had been. Realizing my foolishness, I turned away.

Again! Quick and bright. A single beam of light, like a flashlight turning on, then quickly off again. My heart pounded in my chest. Who was down there?

My eyes searched the darkness. Then I saw it.

It was just a shadow. Near the barn. I could faintly make out the silhouette of something big—an animal of some kind, I was certain. I couldn't tell what I was looking at, though. A deer? No. It was much bigger. With another flash of light, I saw what might be . . . a horse? *What?*

Without a thought, I got up and ran down the stairs. As quickly as I could, I made my way down both sets, big fat brace and all. If my ankle was getting reinjured, I didn't notice.

Dad and Millie were in the living room, so I circled around and entered the kitchen through the dining room. I grabbed my coat near the door and ran out the back.

The light flashed again. I cautiously walked toward it. As I neared the side of the barn, a creature emerged. A horse—maybe. But unlike any horse I had ever seen. It was bigger, with long, lean legs. It had thick, shiny white hair and was slender with a graceful walk that made me think of an elegant ballet dancer prancing around on stage in her pointed shoes. Its eyes glowed brightly in the darkness. They were big, sparkling, and blue. They locked with mine.

Slowly, it began to approach.

"Ellie!" called Dad from the door. "Get back in here!"

The animal was startled by Dad's voice and turned away. Just before it did, I saw the flash of light once more. It seemed to hover above the creature's head. But no, it was coming from the tip . . . of a singular, spiraling horn that stretched long and sharp from its forehead.

The wind whipped around me, and I stood frozen.

It took a whole day to dig ourselves out of the mess that fell that night, and by the time the walkways had been cleared and there was a spot in the driveway for the cars, another storm began its fury.

The weather had pushed the start of school out by another few days, and I was stuck at home waiting . . . *for some kind of life to start already!* I hurled my whiny knot of desperation at the mean universe that kept throwing snowballs at me.

The isolation was on me full and strong and the cabin fever was hot, very hot. No . . . stifling, very stifling. It was too much.

And my extraordinarily gigantic—bigger than the universe—secret wasn't helping. I wanted to tell Peter, but he never called, and I was past the point of thinking he would.

He must have decided for himself that being friends wasn't such a good idea. He had warned me to stay away, after all. Maybe this was his way of pushing me out. I didn't want to be out. But what could I do? I would've gone to search for him at Carle's, but the snow and my ankle said no to that.

So I waited, feverish and hot, for school to finally begin.

Apparently, the kids at Ocean Lake High weren't too accustomed to newcomers, and my first day as the new kid was an uncomfortable ordeal of obtrusive stares and questions, then more stares again.

I didn't mind, though. I was in a good mood. I was finally out of the house and I was eager to at least talk to Peter. I wasn't feeling very hopeful about what he would say, but hearing him say it would be better than the buggy crickets that kept chirping in my ear.

But every time I turned another corner, and every time I entered a new classroom full of unfamiliar faces, I was met with the same thing—no Peter.

He was nowhere. He wasn't even at lunch.

I stood awkwardly in the front of the cafeteria, holding my tray, scanning the room for him. I felt all the eyes on me again and decided on a new tactic.

My brace and I made a clumsy beeline for a free table near the door. I could eat and watch for him at the same time. I had my eye on the door and had just stuffed my face with potatoes when a chair scraped loudly across the floor.

"Is this seat taken?" I looked up to see two girls standing before me. The girl who had spoken was standing with her hand on the back of the chair. She had a heap of dark—almost black—curly hair pulled high on her head. She wore big hooped earrings and a perfectly applied face of rosy makeup over her smooth alabaster skin.

"No," I said, swallowing my mouthful. "Go ahead."

She smiled at me with glossy lips. "I'm Bethany," she said, sitting down beside me. "This is Jenny."

I turned to Jenny, who pulled out a chair in front of me. "Hi, Jenny."

From what I could tell, Jenny wore no makeup, but her olive skin held a natural blush that colored her cheeks, giving her a friendly glow that matched her kind eyes.

"Hi," she said, smoothing a strand of straightened brown hair over her woolen dress.

"What's your name?" asked Bethany.

"I'm Ellie," I said, and before she could ask, I added, "I moved here from New York."

"Oh, really?" said Jenny.

"New York City?" asked Bethany. I nodded. "Did you leave any boyfriends over there?"

"Nope. No boyfriend."

"That's too bad," she said. "There's not much to choose from here." She glanced around the room.

I laughed and scanned the room along with her, not really caring if she was right. "That's okay. I'm not looking for a boyfriend."

"No?" asked Bethany like she was seriously confused.

I shook my head and took a bite of my roll. I thought for a second about mentioning Peter but realized there wasn't really anything to mention. Then I almost asked about him, but I remembered his broken confession about the kids in this town and kept my teeth tight on my tongue.

"Well," said Bethany. "See that kid over there?" She pointed her nose toward a table of red. It was filled with a group of boys wearing the same basketball jerseys as the bullies in Carle's. And they were there, all three of them, talking and laughing in loud, obnoxious bursts. I glared at them.

"Joey Williams sits over there," continued Bethany, not noticing I'd turned foul. "He's the one on the end." She pointed at Joey, who was laughing, *un*-obnoxiously, with a friend at the other end of the table. I thought I recognized him from science. He seemed like an okay kid.

"Don't even think about it," warned Bethany as she saw me looking at Joey. I was about to remind her that she told me to look when she said, "He's Jenny's."

I glanced at Jenny, who dreamingly smiled past me to Joey's table.

"I wouldn't," I said, smiling at her and thinking of Joey Williams's crunchy head of too much gel.

"Oh, and that's Robert Martin. I used to go out with him," said Bethany, pointing at a boy across the room.

She continued to give me full reports on anybody and everybody she knew, along with any unfortunate soul who passed by our table. By the end of lunch, I knew who the losers were, who the popular kids were, and just about everyone who came in between.

Despite the incessant gossiping, I found I liked Bethany and Jenny well enough. We ended up having gym class together after lunch, and Mr. White, our gym teacher, let them sit on the bleachers with me and my injured ankle while the rest of the class played volleyball. And they were both in my last two classes after that as well. Peter wasn't.

I was at my locker, getting ready to close it to the kind of okay, but kind of depressing day. I peered over my shoulder. The kid at his locker beside me looked nice. And he looked quiet. I turned to the boy.

"Hey," I said.

He stared back, confused.

"Hey, do you by any chance know if Peter Evans goes here?" I whispered.

He looked up in thought. "No, I don't think so," he said, shaking his head.

I was just about to start my request for more info when the boy slammed his locker and walked away.

9

"**H**ey!" said Bethany, swinging the door to greet me. Jenny was smiley and happy by her side.

We were having a sleepover at Bethany's. She lived in town, and it wasn't until I showed up at her house that I realized that her apartment was above the strip of stores lining Main Street. And this one, in particular, was right across the street from Carle's Market.

"Ellie!" squealed Jenny. She bounced over to me and grabbed me by the hand, dragging me inside.

"Hey, guys," I said, laughing and feeling pulled in by all the excited energy. They both seemed bubblier and happier out of school. "Here." I handed Bethany a bag of chips to add to our snacks. Of course, I had gone into Carle's to check for Peter; he hadn't been there.

"Thanks," she said, ripping the bag open and moving to the kitchen. She pulled a bowl from a cabinet and emptied the bag. "Do you like scary movies?"

I pulled out a stool. "Sure," I said, smiling and glancing at the

TV in the living room. I was all for a movie but was going to make sure I positioned myself on the couch right next to the big window that looked out onto the street.

"Hey, did she tell you?" asked Jenny, taking a seat. Her smile at me was ecstatic.

"Tell me what," I asked, looking between the two of them with curiosity.

Bethany's eyes popped big and happy. "Alex Anderson asked me out!" she shrieked.

"Which one is he?" I asked, not remembering the name from our lunchtime gossip.

"Alex Anderson," repeated Jenny like it would help me remember. "Only the most popular boy in our class. Cutest, too, if you don't mind me saying." She glanced at Bethany.

"I know, right?" squealed Bethany.

I shrugged, still in the dark. "Guys, that doesn't help."

"You remember," said Jenny. "He sits at the same table as Joey. The kid with the silky blonde hair and blue eyes." She brushed her hands down her hair and batted her eyes at me.

"You mean the tall kid with the loud laugh?" I asked, hoping I was wrong, hoping she wasn't talking about the same kid who I had seen bugging Peter at Carle's.

"Yeah," swooned Bethany. "He is tall, isn't he?" She giggled.

"Yeah," I said, suddenly feeling sick and forgetting to hide the grimace that pulled down my face.

"What?" asked Bethany, noticing my unease.

"Nothing," I said quickly. I pulled my face up. I wasn't sure what I should say. I knew Peter wouldn't want me to tell them about the store and I didn't know how else to explain my problem with her new boyfriend.

"What? You don't like him or something?" Bethany asked.

"No," I said. "It's not that. I just think you can do better."

"Better?" said Jenny and Bethany at the same time.

"It's Alex Anderson, Ellie. There isn't better than Alex Anderson," snorted Bethany.

"Yeah, there is," I said.

"Like who?" she asked.

"Anybody," I said, raising my arms like it should be obvious.

Bethany's jaw dropped. "What, are you jealous?"

"No, I'm not jealous, I just—"

"You sound jealous." She snorted again.

I was appalled. I shot her a look of disgust and was about to let her know that I absolutely was not jealous, that she could have that bully Alex Anderson, and that . . .

"Okay, okay," said Jenny, who was getting blasted by our steamy glares.

Bethany and I turned our hard eyes to Jenny. I relaxed my tight jaw.

"Let's just go watch the movie," she scolded. She picked up the bowl of chips and headed to the couch, leaving me and Bethany to fume at each other.

I composed myself, realizing with shame I was being ridiculous. "Sorry, Bethany," I said. "I didn't mean anything by it. I just . . ."

"Fine," she said. She huffed on her way past me and into the living room, then sat on the couch, taking my seat near the window.

"What's the matter?" asked Millie. She was standing in the doorway, staring at me.

"What?" I glanced over at Millie but failed to meet her eyes. I turned back to the blank TV in front of me. I had come home from school and plopped down on the couch, intending to watch something, but now I was just staring at the black screen with the remote lax in my hand. "Nothing," I said, pressing at the button to turn it on.

Millie moved into the room and sat down beside me. "Is everything okay?"

"Yeah." I sighed. "I'm just ready to get this thing off already." I kicked my braced foot out in front of me.

"I'm taking you tomorrow."

"Yeah, I know. I'm just tired of it."

"Is that it?" she asked, sounding concerned. "How's school going?"

"School's school," I said as I shuffled through some movies. I wasn't really in the mood to talk.

"How are your friends?" asked Millie. Me not wanting to talk meant she was going to keep bugging me until I did.

I stopped clicking and twisted my neck to look at her. "Good," I said. "I'm fine. Really."

I was fine, but I wasn't feeling very happy these days. Bethany had been going out with Alex for three weeks now. I had talked to her again the day after our fight and tried to apologize. We kind of made amends, but I felt some irreparable damage had been done and I was sorry for it. It hadn't been my intention to hurt her. I was actually concerned for her, but I had done a poor job of showing it that night. School with Bethany and Jenny was now an uncomfortable mess of tension and tightrope-walking.

"Have you heard from Peter?"

I perked up a little but quickly flattened again. "No, but that's okay. It wasn't really anything."

"That's a shame," said Millie, patting my knee. She smiled. "You know what I think we should do?" she asked, her voice rising in pitch.

Oh no. I was scared. That tone could only mean one thing.

"Movie night!" she shouted happily. "Just me and you. Tomorrow. Okay? Doesn't that sound like fun?"

"I guess."

"Oh, come on," she said gleefully. "It'll be fun! Okay?"

"It's a date," I said, trying to force a smile.

She patted me on the shoulder and got up. "A date!" she called back happily from the kitchen.

To my surprise, movie night with Millie was exactly what I needed.

We rented our favorite Disney flick, *Sleeping Beauty*, and

ordered Chinese food. Then we let the movie play in the background while we chatted about life.

Maybe it was the freedom from finally having my brace removed, but I surprised even myself with how much I had to say, and I ended up spilling my guts to her—about everything, things I didn't even know I was feeling.

I talked mostly about Peter. I was heartbroken and sad and angry and very annoyed with myself for feeling any of those things over a boy I had only known for one day.

I also told her about the situation at school with the girls and about what I saw with Alex and Peter at the store. Millie was understanding and easy to talk to like always, and I woke up the next day feeling much better than I had in a while.

It was seriously such a relief, and I was ready to stop the useless moping and get on with my life. The sun was shining through my window and the spring morning looked lovely and bright. It was going to be a great day.

I pushed open the door, inhaling the fresh Saturday morning air. It was crisp and cool, and there was a light dusting of snow on the ground—perfect.

I reached around the door to the kitchen and grabbed my coat from the hook. Without my brace, I could now be out here in the snow and mud without Dad fussing.

I walked to the edge of the barn, where I had seen the mythical creature. I made a few sweeps around the grounds, trying to spot footprints in the freshly laid fluff. My tracking skills needed some work, though, because I had yet to even find any squirrel's tracks, and I *knew* I had seen them hopping around out here earlier.

There had been no other sightings of magical creatures since the night of the storm, but my restless mind was not letting it go. I wanted to at least know what I had seen, and if I could find some tracks, maybe I would be able to identify the animal they belonged to.

I was deep in thought, making yet another pass around the barn when the buzz of my phone startled me. I reached for my pocket.

I didn't recognize the number.

"Hello," I said.

"Can I come over?"

It was Peter.

I waited on the porch for Peter. His footsteps scuffled on the pebbled drive. My heart skipped in my chest and I quietly scolded myself for it. I didn't want to get so worked up over this kid again, but here I was, nervous and feeling happy.

I walked down to meet him. He looked up at me and summoned a feeble smile.

"Here," he said. He held out his hand. It was a candy necklace with pretty pink pastel pieces forming the chain and a heart pendant hanging from its center, reminding me of my grandmother's locket. "Don't worry, I'm still going to buy you something better. This is just . . ." He paused. "Just an . . . I'm sorry . . . I guess," he said. "Anyway." He reached up and placed the necklace around my neck. I pulled my hair through the strand and centered the heart on my chest.

I glanced back up at Peter. He looked sad and defeated and altogether like a big miserable mess.

He stared at me with his good but very sad eyes.

"So you don't go to my school, do you?" I asked.

He laughed. "No, I don't." He paused and stared at me for a second. "I'm homeschooled."

"Oh my god! Homeschool! I didn't think of that." I shook my head. "You know I searched the whole school for you?"

He shrugged. "Sorry, I forgot to tell you."

"You also forgot to call me," I said, gently kicking his toe.

He tilted his head to one side. "I didn't forget," he said with a weak smile.

"So where have you been?"

He stared at the ground and pushed some pebbles around with his feet. "My dad came back," he said. "It's been a little crazy at home."

"Are you okay?"

He glanced up at me uncomfortably. "Yeah, can we not talk about it right now, though?" He pulled in a deep breath, trying to stifle the tears I already saw.

I nodded quietly and chewed on my lip. I fixed my eyes on the barn behind him, thinking maybe a little of my unicorn delirium would cheer him up.

"Do you want to help me with something?" I asked.

"Sure," he said. "What's up?"

I smiled at him. "Do you know anything about tracking?"

"I'm not crazy."

"I didn't say you were."

"It's in your eyes," I said.

Peter smiled. "Look, if you say you saw a unicorn, I believe you."

"Good. Now come help me track it."

He got up from the steps and followed me to the barn.

We paced around, tracing the same steps from my failed mission earlier. But Peter was better at this tracking stuff and was able to point out a squirrel's, a cat's, and a deer's tracks. We didn't find any unicorn prints, however.

"We don't really know what they look like," Peter reminded me. "And they're magical. They might not leave prints."

"True, true," I said. "But there aren't any horse prints here or anything?"

"No," said Peter, scanning the ground again.

I chewed on my cheek. "I was hoping I'd find something that made sense."

"You really think you saw one, don't you?"

"Eh . . . I don't know," I said, feeling a little stupid. "I saw something. That's all."

"What did your dad say?"

I wobbled a little. "Oh, he says it was a deer, but . . ." I thought for a second. "Yeah, I guess it was probably just a deer."

Peter's stomach growled.

"I think your stomach's telling us to take a break. Want some lunch?"

He put a hand to his belly. "Sure," he said.

Dad and Millie were talking in the kitchen when we entered. Millie always made a big dinner on Saturdays and was already busy chopping away at some carrots. Casual weekend Dad sat beside her with a beer in his hand.

Their heads turned when they noticed I wasn't alone.

"Hey, Dad. You remember Peter."

"How's it going, son?" asked Dad.

Millie put her knife down, wiped her hands on her apron, and walked over to us with a big smile on her face.

"Peter!" she gushed. "It's so good to finally meet you." She stretched out her hand and shook Peter's vigorously. "I have heard so much about you."

"Peter, this is Millie. I'm sorry. I may have told her a little about you."

I hadn't really been serious with my apology and was surprised to see Peter roll frustrated eyes at me before turning back to Millie.

"Hi, nice to meet you." He smiled at Millie politely and nodded to Dad. "Sir," he said.

"Call me Jim," Dad said.

I opened the fridge and pulled out the leftover Chinese food. I threw it in the microwave, then grabbed some forks from the drawer. "Is it okay if we hang out in my room?" I asked.

"Absolutely not!" boomed Dad.

"Okay, okay!" I said, stepping off the toes I hadn't meant to stomp on.

Dad narrowed his gaze sternly. "Your room is in the attic, Ellie. He will never see your room."

"They're just kids, Jim," said Millie, trying to help us out.

"Nope. Not gonna happen." Dad was shaking his head.

"We'll just hang out in the *living room*?" I questioned, unsure now if this would be okay.

"That's better," said Dad. "You staying for dinner, Peter?"

"No, I don't want to be any trouble, but thanks."

"No trouble," said Dad.

"Oh, come on, stay!" I pleaded. Peter met me with rolled eyes again, but this time they just looked tired and were back to being sad.

I turned to Dad and Millie. "We'll let you guys know."

The microwave dinged, and I pulled out the food.

"All right," said Dad. "There'll be plenty if you want."

"Yeah, I'm making my famous shepherd's pie," said Millie. "There's going to be too much for us—there always is. I can wrap some up for your mom, too. We'll just end up tossing it."

"Thanks, yeah, that'd be great," said Peter.

"I didn't come here looking for handouts," huffed Peter. He slumped onto the couch in a puff of steam.

"Wow," I said. I was stopped in a squat with my knees bent, just about to sit beside him.

I stared down at Peter on the couch. He was folded over his knees with his hands—clenched and stressed—grabbing tightly at his messy hair.

I finished sitting and put the food on the coffee table.

"I'm sorry," he mumbled. His voice was low and muffled and I could barely hear it, but I did.

I nudged him with my elbow. "It's okay."

He sniffed. I pulled out a tissue from a box on the end table and tucked it under his arm.

"I can just go," he said, grabbing at the tissue. He sat up and leaned against the couch. "I shouldn't have come over like this."

"Don't go. You can be like this. It's fine."

He smiled at me weakly, then stared off somewhere far.

"Was it what Millie said?" I asked.

His red eyes rolled up a little. "Not really."

"She's like my mom, Peter. You can't get mad at me for talking to her."

"Yeah, I know," he said. "I'm not. It's just . . ."

"What?"

He struggled to meet my eyes.

"What?" I repeated.

"What about at school?" he asked finally. He shifted back to his knees and stared at the floor.

"What about school?"

"I suppose you've been talking about me at school, too?" he mumbled at the ground.

"No," I said to the back of his head. "No, I haven't. They don't even know I know you."

Peter sat up, staring at me with narrowed eyes. "Really?" he asked like he didn't believe me.

I shot my head back a little, offended that he'd think I was lying.

"Sorry," he said. "It's just I saw you with Bethany and Jenny at Carle's last week and I just thought . . . I don't know." He pressed his hands to his eyes and let out a weary sigh. "Sorry, I've kinda been in my own head, and I forgot how nice you were and—" He glanced at me and stopped.

I was glaring at him.

"What?" he asked.

"You saw me in town? And you didn't say anything?"

"I'm sorry. I can't talk to them. And I didn't want to embarrass you." He looked at me apologetically.

I shook my head at him. "Didn't we talk about this already?"

He shrugged and closed his eyes. He fell back against the couch and was quiet.

"No," I said.

He opened them again and met my gaze. "No?"

I was shaking my head. "Yeah. No. If we're going to be friends, you can't keep doing that. I'm not embarrassed by you, so get over it. You know I thought you were going to be at school, right?" He looked up, thinking about that. "Yeah," I said. "And I wish you were there."

"Yeah?" he asked, sounding hopeful.

"God yeah." I sighed. "School kind of sucks. Do you think your mom would let you come?"

Peter laughed. "No thanks," he said, laughing again. "But thanks."

A feeble smile pulled on his lips, but he looked down again, and it faded.

"Here," I said, moving the food across the coffee table. I handed him a fork. "Eat. You'll feel better."

"So is the unicorn the only thing I missed?" asked Peter with a bite of noodles.

I chewed on my food, trying to think. "Um . . . well, you missed my broken foot."

"No, I was there for that."

"You didn't get to see the ugly brace, though."

"Oh really? Sorry," said Peter, glancing down at my stockinged feet. "It looks better now."

I smiled at him. "Yeah, it's better."

I put my food down and crossed my legs on the couch. I bit my lip tentatively, staring at him. "So why *were* you gone?" I asked. I knew he wasn't going to want to talk about it, but I also got the feeling I would never know if I didn't ask.

He sighed and put down his food. "Ah . . . well, my dad's an ass, basically," he said.

"Do you want to elaborate?"

Peter slumped back on the couch. It took him a minute. "Um . . . so it was that night after I left here, actually," he said, glancing over at me. "I was babysitting my little brother, and my dad showed up totally wasted. He's been gone for months . . . and he just shows up out of nowhere.

"Anyway, he was yelling and trying to take Liam. I didn't know what to do, so I called the cops and . . . well, he had Liam in the car when the cops arrived, and he got arrested.

"And then they opened an investigation on my mom. I don't even know why, but we had to stay at my grandma's for a couple of weeks. She lives a few hours away, so that's where I've been, mostly."

"Damn," I said. I stared at the tissue clenched tightly in Peter's hands, still taking in the loaded story. "So you weren't purposely avoiding me this whole time?" I asked, trying to lighten the mood.

LIGHTS AT MIDNIGHT

He laughed. "No, that I was not." He smiled weakly. "And sorry about tonight. It's just . . . my mom's been such a mess. I had to get out of there. I didn't know I was going to be like this."

"It's okay," I said. Peter's doubtful eyes rolled up. "Really . . . you're fine." I slumped on the couch beside him and bumped his shoulder with mine. "And I'm sorry. That all sucks."

"Thanks," he said, bumping me back. He closed his eyes again.

I observed him for a second, trying to think of something to get his mind off things. I got up and grabbed the PlayStation controllers from the TV stand. "I hope you like *Fortnite*," I said, handing him the controller.

༄

Peter and I played games until dinner. Then we sat on the floor, eating at the coffee table while we watched a movie.

I gave him control of the remote and laughed when he got excited over an anime *Godzilla* movie he found on Netflix. It was in Japanese with English subtitles, and it took all my concentration to follow along and eat my dinner at the same time.

I was fixated on the screen when Peter gently poked my hand with his fork. "Earth to Ellie."

I turned to him, not realizing I'd been lost in a world of spaceships and monsters for a while.

"I should probably get going," he said.

"Oh really?" I put my fork down, frowning. "What time is it?"

"I don't know. Late, I think."

"Can't you stay a little longer?"

He smiled at me, then moved to the couch and lay down. "I'll stay until your dad kicks me out."

I got up and pulled the throw over him, then sat cross-legged at the opposite end. Peter stretched out his feet and tucked them under mine, and something soft fluttered in my stomach.

We continued to watch the movie in silence for a while. Then, out of nowhere, Peter turned to me. "Thanks," he said with a yawn.

I stared at him, confused. "What are you thanking me for?"

"Just, you know, for today, for being here." He paused. "For being so nice."

I smiled. "I told you you can trust me."

"Yeah," he said, his eyes drooping. "I'm starting to see that." Another yawn escaped him.

"Are you tired?"

"Nah, I'm okay. I'm just resting." His eyes closed at that, and I thought he had dropped off. "Hey, Ellie," said Peter, his eyes still closed. "You're perfect, ya know?"

I laughed. "Was that the cheesy thing you wanted to tell me from before?"

"Something like that," he said with a sleepy smile.

I laughed again, tossing a pillow at him. He grabbed it and hugged it tight to his chest, still smiling.

The living room door swung open. It was Dad.

"Ellie, it's gettin' late."

I glanced at Peter, who was now drifting away somewhere in dreamland. "Can he stay?" I asked.

Dad grappled for a moment with the decision. He looked at the sleeping Peter, then back to me with a reluctant nod. "You better get off to bed, though."

I got up and spread the blanket more evenly across Peter. "Night, Peter," I said and patted his head.

12

"Hey, Ellie!" Somewhere in the distance, someone was calling my name. I slowly drifted up, back to my bed, and into my room.

It was morning. Bright sunlight was shining at me through my window. My sleep had been deep and sound, and it took a moment for last night to come back to me, but then I remembered—Peter was back, and he was here. A smile bloomed on my face.

"Hey, Ellie! Wake up!"

"Just a second!" I hurried out of bed. Peter was standing by my door at the bottom of the stairs. "What are you doing up here? My dad!"

"He said it was okay, as long as I don't go up there. Now, come on! I need to show you something."

"All right, all right. I'll be down in a second!"

I pulled some clothes from my drawer and quickly got dressed. I moved to the mirror and ran a comb through my hair. I licked my hand and tried to tame a pesky piece, then frowned at my results.

Oh well. It would have to do. I popped a stick of gum into my mouth, then paused to center my new candy necklace. I smiled and hurried down the stairs.

Peter was waiting for me at the bottom.

"Hey, Peter. You're at my house," I said, awkwardly stating the obvious.

"Yeah." He laughed. "Thanks for letting me stay and uh . . . for putting up with me last night."

"No problem," I said, playfully punching his shoulder. "So what do you have to show me?"

"I found one." There was a cute glint in his eyes.

"What? Really?" My mouth fell open. Peter smiled, big and happy. He grabbed my hand. "Come on, I'll show you."

"Just over here."

Peter led me to the side of the barn where the snow had receded a little. He pointed at some frozen mud, but there was nothing to see. I was about to tell him we had just checked this spot yesterday when he moved and changed the position of his shadow.

In the sunlight, I could distinctly make out the curved shape of a very large hoofprint. I squatted down to get a better look. Peter knelt beside me.

"So it *was* real," I said faintly. "This is unbelievable! And this definitely isn't a deer's track?"

"No. No way. Deer have cloven hooves. They'd be much smaller than this, anyway. Not a moose, either. And if it's a horse, it's a pretty big horse."

"This is crazy, huh?" I asked, trying to make sense of it.

"Yep. Nuts," he agreed.

Well, that was good. At least I could hang on to the fact that we both agreed this was absolutely and irrefutably bonkers.

I looked at Peter with a big grin I couldn't hold back.

"When can you come over?" I asked Peter. He was sitting at the kitchen island, munching on a bowl of cereal.

He shrugged. "Whenever," he said with a bite.

"So, Saturday?"

"Sure."

I had decided a stakeout was in order. We would conceal ourselves in a tent while luring the creature in with food. The perfect plan.

We were strategizing in the kitchen. I was, at least. Peter seemed more interested in the cereal box on the counter in front of him. I opened the fridge to check for carrots—nothing.

"Millie!" I shouted across the house. "Do we have any carrots?" I opened the vegetable crisper, but everything was green.

"No, I don't think so, hon," Millie called back from the living room.

"That's okay," I said to the room because Peter wasn't paying attention to me anymore. "It's better if they're fresh," I decided as

I continued to talk to the kitchen. I turned to Peter. "Can you pick some up on your way over?"

"What?"

"The carrots!" I kind of shouted.

"Mmkay," he said, grinning at me with a mouth full of milky Cheerios.

We spent the rest of the week planning for the stakeout. There really wasn't much to it, so we just met each day with the plan to plan, then hung out and played video games instead. I waited for Peter at the lake the following Saturday—the day of the Secret Unicorn Mission. That was what I was calling it.

The spring days kept bouncing back and forth between cold and a little less cold, and the ice on the lake was holding firm. I was standing at the end of the dock, staring at the frozen water wistfully, wishing I could jump in.

"Boo," called Peter from behind me.

"Hey," I said, turning to face him. I had heard him creeping up. "Did you get them?"

"What?"

"The carrots!" I scolded impatiently.

Peter lifted the two drinks he was holding—they weren't carrots. "Sorry, I forgot," he said, handing me a drink.

I shook my head with a smile; he did look sorry. "That's okay. We can still go. Do you want to head over now?"

Peter nodded, and we started toward the street.

I took a sip of the hot drink. "Where did you get hot chocolate?"

"The diner," he said. "My mom's working."

"Oh." I took another sip. "What about Liam?"

"He's staying at my grandmother's so my mom can work. The weekends are busier. Better tips."

"Hey, I can babysit if she needs a babysitter," I suggested. "She wouldn't need to pay me."

Peter shook his head. "No way. I found you first."

"Oh, come on. I really want to meet your family . . . especially your cute baby brother."

Peter was still shaking his head. "It wouldn't work. Your dad wouldn't even let you over there without my mom, and then I'd have to go to your house to prove I wasn't there. It wouldn't make any sense. We would just be swapping houses."

"You got to let me meet them someday."

"I know," Peter said with a sulk.

We passed the diner on our way to Carle's, but I didn't mention going in to see his mom like I wanted to.

We entered the store and found the microscopic produce section. I spotted the carrots and picked up a bag.

"What about apples?" suggested Peter.

"Do you think they like apples?"

"Honestly, I don't know," he said.

"If it's not a horse . . . maybe it doesn't eat what horses eat." This was just occurring to me.

"Yeah," said Peter. "But it's our best bet, right?"

"Right," I agreed.

Peter picked up the big bag of way too many apples. "Do you think this will be enough?" he asked dryly.

I laughed. "Hey, if this doesn't work, I can make an apple pie. Oh, or apple crisp!" I exclaimed, getting excited about the idea.

"Ah, man, I love apple crisp," said Peter. He put a hand to his stomach. "You can't say apple crisp in front of me."

"Well, now I know what I'm going to do with the apples," I said with a laugh.

We found our way to the register and were waiting in line when someone called my name. I turned around. Bethany and Jenny were walking up to me with two girls from school whom I recognized from math class.

"Oh, hey, guys," I said.

"Hey, Ellie," said Bethany with a sideways glance at Peter. "What are you up to today?"

The two girls from math stared in Peter's direction. One girl leaned into the other and whispered something in her ear and they both giggled. I glared at them.

"Me and Peter are hanging out," I said.

Peter had fallen behind and was excluding himself from the circle that had now formed. I took a step back to include him.

"Do you guys know Peter?" I asked, giving him a friendly pat on the back.

"Yeah, Peter Evans," said Jenny. "You used to go to my church. Hi."

"Hey," said Peter, glancing up at Jenny shyly.

"So how do you two know each other?" asked Bethany, scanning Peter with an unapproving eye.

I crossed my arms and scowled at her. I didn't like the way she was looking at him, and I didn't care for her condescending tone, either.

"Peter's my boyfriend," I said, knowing it would cause a bit of a stir among them.

There was a scuffle from Peter, who had perked up and was now staring at me.

"Oh yeah?" queried Bethany.

She looked back and forth between Peter and me, her gaze pokey and annoyingly judgy.

"Yeah." I stared her down.

A retort formed on her lips, but she held back.

"Well, we need to head out," I said, knowing it would be wise to get away before Bethany or I started up again.

"Okay," said Bethany. "See you later."

She and the other two girls walked off while Jenny lingered behind.

"Sorry," said Jenny. "Alex broke up with her. She's been on edge."

"Oh, really?" I said, now feeling like an awful friend. "What happened?"

"Let's just say you were right. He's no good."

"Is she okay?"

"Yeah, she'll be fine." She looked at me with a friendly smile. "Hey, I'm having a birthday party at my house in a couple of weeks. You guys should come. Both of you," she said to Peter.

"Thanks, Jenny." I smiled back. "That would be great."

"Okay. Well, see you Monday," she said, turning to meet back up with Bethany.

Peter and I were just outside the store, filling my backpack with our unicorn bate. He hoisted the bag onto his shoulder and looked at me with a big smile on his face.

"What?" I asked.

"So I'm your boyfriend?" His smile was sly and pathetic. And very cute.

I shook my head, feeling embarrassed. "Oh, no, Peter, I just said that to get them to lay off you."

"Nope. You can't take it back now," said Peter, grinning widely.

"What? No, Peter. It's okay. I just—"

"Ah . . . this is gonna be great," he said, paying me no mind. "You know, I've never had a girlfriend before."

"In your dreams," I said, rolling my eyes, but I couldn't hold back a happy smile.

"What's going on here?" asked Dad.

I had pulled the tent from the basement and was carrying it when I entered the kitchen. Dad was sitting at the table, sipping a cup of coffee.

"Stakeout," I reminded him.

Dad narrowed his eyes at me. "What are you doing with a tent?"

I stopped and cautiously looked at him. "Uh . . . Peter and I are going to camp out in the yard and wait for it?" I explained as a question because I was asking now for the first time.

Dad was shaking his head.

"Come on, Dad!" I begged. "It's too cold to sit out there."

"Ellie," he warned.

"Please, Dad."

He sighed and put down his coffee. "The porch," he said. "Next to this window." He tapped at the window beside him.

I smiled. "Thanks, Dad."

I happily headed outside with the tent.

"Unicorns!" I shouted gleefully to Peter, who was waiting on the porch.

Dad bellowed behind me, solemn and grumpy, "It was just a deer."

꙳

"Okay, so . . . the apples and carrots are in the backpack, and Millie gave me some celery and strawberries." I had the Tupperware in my hands to show Peter. I placed them next to the backpack.

We were on the porch, just outside Dad's window, snug and cozy inside the tent. I stuffed in as many extra pillows and blankets as I could find, and we sat toasty and warm under the fluff as we watched eagerly out the mesh-screened windows.

"So what's the plan if we see it?" I asked, my words piping out as steamy vapor when I spoke.

"I don't know." Peter shrugged. "I hadn't thought that far."

"Ha, me neither," I said. We had spent all week planning for tonight but hadn't even considered what we would do if we actually spotted a unicorn. "I suppose that neither of us think we're really going to see anything, huh?"

"Maybe not," he agreed.

"That's okay. We can just hang out."

I twisted around and reached for a container I had packed for us. "I have dinner if you're hungry," I said, opening it. "It's a Frito pie. I made it for Dad. He's from Texas and loves himself a good ol' Frito pie." I handed Peter a spoon. "I saw him trying to make it at a gas station with the cheese and chili machines once, and I've been making it for him ever since."

Peter laughed and went for a bite. "Oh, wait, I forgot." I pulled out a bag of corn chips and sprinkled a bunch on top. I nudged him the go-ahead. "I didn't want them to get soggy," I explained.

He took a big crunchy bite and smiled. "Mmm," he moaned happily. He chewed more enthusiastically. "Really good," he said, swallowing his bite.

I handed him a bottle of water.

"So you're part New Yorker and part Texan?" Peter asked, taking a sip.

"Yeah," I said. "Well, Dad was never really much of a New Yorker and he raised me, so sometimes I feel like I am." I pushed a messy spoonful into my mouth, then grabbed for a napkin, handing one to Peter. "I'm pretty sure we would have been following Millie back to Tennessee soon if this hadn't come up." I gestured around the tent but meant the outside and Maine and everything that wasn't New York.

"Did you like New York?"

"I loved it," I said, thinking back fondly. "It's really pretty great there. It's bigger, yet somehow it felt cozier. This here"—I gestured to the tent again—"it's so desolate. It makes you feel unprotected and forsaken or something . . . you know?"

Peter nodded. "Some people like that."

"Dad does." I smiled.

"What about you?" he asked. "Do you wish you could go back?"

I shook my head. "No, New York was great, but . . ." I paused and smiled again. I went forward with my thought. "But . . . it didn't have a Peter Evans."

Peter smiled slyly. "You know, it probably did have a Peter Evans."

I scowled at him and tried to kick him under the blankets, but a pillow was in the way.

"So what happened to your mom?" he asked.

"She died during childbirth. Hemorrhaging or something. I don't really know. I guess it was pretty horrific and sad. Dad doesn't talk about it."

"Geez . . . that's awful. I'm sorry. I didn't think girls died during childbirth anymore," said Peter with a pained expression.

I shrugged. "Yeah, I feel guilty about it sometimes. Like . . . I feel like I need to be something special in order to make up for it. I mean, she basically gave her life up for me." I let out an anxious breath. "And the pressure's real." And now that I was talking about it, I felt it. *Oh boy.*

Peter put his spoon down. "You are special, Ellie."

I rolled my eyes at him.

"No," he contended. He held my gaze. "That's what I was going to say before. You and Granny Leira. Both of you. You have the same . . ." He stopped to think. "I don't know. . . *Light* that makes you shine. But you're even brighter than she was." He shook his head and pressed his lips tight, like he was trying to work something out. "I don't know what it is, but . . . you radiate like a star or something."

My heart skipped. "Did you just say that to me?"

If I was a star, I was falling.

"Told you it was cheesy," he said, looking down, embarrassed.

"Oh my god, Peter," I said, kicking him under the blankets again and feeling like I was actually going to cry. I found his stockinged feet this time and tapped my foot on his. "That's not cheesy—that's freakin' adorable." I wiped at the corners of my eyes because I *was* crying.

I looked at Peter, shaking my head and feeling myself floating away. I came back down and focused. I stared at Peter staring back at me. "So what about you?" I asked.

"What about me?"

"Tell me about your life here."

He frowned. "Eh . . . I don't want to talk about my life. It's boring. You already know everything."

I frowned back and realized I needed to be more specific or else I wouldn't be getting anything out of him. "Okay," I said. "Tell me something I don't know. What about Liam? How old is he?"

Peter answered easily. "Liam's one and a half."

"Do you have the same dad?"

He nodded.

"So your parents are recently divorced?"

He squirmed in his seat a little. "They're not actually divorced. He was kinda just gone one day. It was right before Liam was born." Peter squirmed again and fiddled with his hands. "My mom says he had a tough childhood, which is why he drinks, but he can't handle it. It's not like with your dad, where he has a couple of beers and he's done. My dad always takes it to the next level—and it changes him."

"What's he like when he's not drinking?"

Peter looked sad when he answered. "He's cool when he's not drinking . . . a totally different person."

I found his foot again and wiggled my toes against it. "Sorry," I said.

Peter tried a weak smile, but it fell. "Yeah, we used to be kinda close, actually. I feel bad for Liam because he basically doesn't have a dad."

"He's got a great big brother," I said, pushing on Peter's foot again. "So how come you think everybody hates you?"

"Because they do." He stared at the pillows. "You saw how they were at the store. That's my life here in Ocean Lake."

I wobbled my head because he was right. I *had* seen it, and not just with Bethany. "Okay, how come, though? It seems a little ridiculous to me."

"Ah, well . . ." said Peter reluctantly. "He's made more than a few scenes over at Mikey's in town and . . . I guess he kinda had a fling with some married woman here. It got around and everyone blasted him for it. She was a mom of some jock kid here, so I got blasted for it, too."

I felt my skin burning. "That's completely unfair."

Peter shrugged.

"So is that why your mom kicked him out?"

"Ha . . ." said Peter with a bit of a smile. "Yeah, she probably did kick him out, but I don't know, honestly." He sounded tired and his eyes peering back looked tired. "Hey, can we not talk about this anymore?"

"All right," I said, wavering a little. I wanted to keep talking, but . . . "Yeah, okay. Sorry." I chewed on my lip, trying to think of something to squelch all the other questions I had for him. "Hey, why don't we play a game?"

"Okay. What kind of game?"

I thought for a second. "How about Never Have I Ever?"

"Okay," said Peter. "I'm not sure how to play."

"It's fun. I'll show you." I grabbed one of Millie's Tupperware. "So we'll use these strawberries. We each get ten." I divided the strawberries into two empty solo cups. "I'm gonna say never have I ever and then something that I have never done before. But if you *have* done it, you have to eat one of your strawberries."

"I don't really like strawberries that much," grumbled Peter.

"Well, good. That'll make it more interesting."

He sulked. I ignored him and continued to explain.

"Whoever is left with the most strawberries at the end wins. Got it?"

"Yeah, okay."

"Okay, I'll go first." I thought for a second. "Never have I ever . . . cheated on a test."

I waited for Peter's response. I wasn't all that surprised when he went for the strawberry. He popped it into his mouth and put up his arms, feigning innocence. "Hey, my mom left the answers on the table right next to me." He shrugged. "I don't think I was the one to blame there."

"Yeah right, I already know you're a cheater." I laughed, remembering his Skittle toss performance at the lake. "Okay, your turn."

Peter thought for a second, then said, "Never have I ever . . . peed in a pool."

"Ooh, gross. No, never." I laughed.

"Am I supposed to eat a strawberry if I've done it?" asked Peter.

"Oh my god, Peter. TMI!" I shouted through giggles as I tossed a pillow at his face. The pillow struck him harder than I had meant, and it rebounded and hit me in the head. We both broke out in a fit of laughter that rolled in waves as we replayed the awkward moment in our minds.

"Okay, okay. I've got one," I said after we had recovered enough to go on. Peter was still wheezing a little when I spoke. "Never have I ever . . . been kissed."

Peter gulped and looked at me now with a sober face. His strawberry remained untouched.

"Me neither," I said.

"But . . . I kissed you down by the dock, remember?"

"Oh, come on, that didn't count. Wasn't even on the lips." I swallowed a lump in my throat. "Do you want to?" I asked. "You know, just to see what it's like."

Peter laughed quietly.

"What?" I asked.

"That's not why I would want to kiss you."

I smiled. "That's okay," I said, completely in agreement with that.

Peter pressed his lips together tightly. "I don't know, Ellie. Your dad's right in there." He pointed at the mesh screen and to the open kitchen window.

"He's in the living room. He won't see," I whispered.

Peter sighed, looking torn.

"It's okay," I said. "It was probably a bad idea, anyway." I stared at my cup of strawberries, trying to hide my disappointment.

"No, wait," said Peter. He shifted in his pile of pillows uncomfortably. "Okay." He settled.

"Yeah?" I smiled happily.

"Yeah." He nodded, taking a nervous breath. "Let's make this quick, though. I don't want your—"

"Yeah, yeah, I know," I said hastily, wishing he would leave Dad out of it.

"Okay," said Peter again.

We sat for a minute, staring at each other in silence.

"Your move," I whispered.

He nodded but didn't budge.

"I thought you said you were going to be quick."

"Don't rush me. I'm thinking."

"What are you thinking about? Just do—"

"Hush," said Peter, putting a finger to my lips.

I was quiet.

He leaned forward and lingered with our noses slightly touching and tickling a little. He was so close I could smell the men's-section shampoo in his hair and could hear the breath I saw piping white and steamy through his nose.

"You sure?" he asked.

"Yeah." My voice was a whisper.

He smiled a little, then pressed his lips to mine. They were soft . . . and warm . . . and sweet . . . and so good . . . and I didn't want him to take them away.

He pulled them from me and sat back down quietly. "How was that?" he asked.

"Good," I said with a small gasp because I might have stopped breathing. "Your lips are soft like strawberries." I put my fingers to my lips, remembering.

"Yours too," he said with a smile and a wiggle of his toes with mine.

I stared back at Peter and had to bite my lip to stop from smiling too much.

"Um, so do you want to keep playing?" I asked. My oxygen was returning and the blush on my cheeks was heating up. "It's your turn," I said with a coaxing hand to get him to *just go already*.

"Yeah, okay," he said with a small chuckle. "Um, let me think for a second . . . Okay, I got one. Never have I ever . . ." He paused.

I sat waiting for his response, but he was quiet. "Hurry up," I pestered.

Peter didn't speak but stared past me vacantly.

"What?"

"Seen . . . a . . . unicorn." The words formed on his lips, but his voice was vapor. He lifted a finger and pointed outside the tent.

I turned.

There, in the wide-open, just stepping out of the woods from the same trail Peter and I had walked on our very first day together, stood a large, white, and very real unicorn.

"Ellie, what are you doing?"

This was the part of the night we hadn't planned for, but now, in the moment, I knew it didn't matter. I heard Peter, but his voice was a weak whisper in some distant place, far from the new, narrowed focus of my mind.

I was pulling on my boots, with my hand on the zipper, looking out the screen door to the strange white creature that stood, elegant and poised, in my backyard.

It was staring at me. It was calling to me. I didn't hear it. I felt it—a gentle tug on my heart, and I needed to go.

I unzipped the tent.

"Ellie," tried Peter again.

I turned back to him. "Hey, give me an apple," I said. "I'm going out there."

Peter reached into the bag and pulled one out. I made a grab for it. He yanked his hand back and shot me a concerned look. "I'm coming with you," he snapped.

"Okay, come," I snapped back impatiently.

The night air was cold on my skin, but adrenaline pulsed and warmed my veins.

The unicorn was plainly visible in the moonlight. We crossed under the cover of a large oak tree, and in the bright, full light of the moon, so were we. It fixed its eyes on us and gracefully stepped forward.

I ambled toward it, the frozen snow crunching under my boots with each step.

"Ellie, be careful." Peter's shaky voice trailed behind.

"It's okay," I called back, fearless and resolute. With the tug on my heart came a sense of calm. I was steady and sure and perfectly at peace with letting this strange creature lure me.

I came to a stop, leaving just a few feet remaining between me and the giant beast. It stopped and grunted softly with flaring nostrils, its breath hot and steamy in the frosty air.

The unicorn gazed at me with kind, unthreatening eyes that made me feel safe. I knew instantly, with no worries at all, that this creature had no ill intentions. And instead, a lovely sense of comfort and warmth came over me as I stood beside it in the bitter night.

I gazed at the creature standing magnificently in front of me. I was awestruck. I wasn't sure, but I thought it might be the same one I had seen on the night of the storm. It stared at me with the same crystal blue eyes.

It was big. Enormous. Growing up in the city, I never really got to see too many horses, but I imagined it was probably even bigger than some of the large Clydesdales I'd seen on TV.

Of course, this wasn't a horse at all.

It stood in the open with the moonlight shining down on a beautiful, stark white coat—thick and glistening in the blue beams. Its mane was a medium gray, with shiny, metallic silver strands catching in the light and falling down its neck in long, wavy tendrils. A silver horn, matching the color of its mane, stretched out long and sharp from its forehead, piercing the night sky.

"Hey there," I said.

It stared at me with big eyes lined heavily in black.

I took a tentative step forward. It showed no signs of fear, and I closed the space between us. I stretched out my hand, finding an urge to touch the softness of its mane. It turned its head and nuzzled its nose against my shoulder.

"Hey," I said again, a nervous laugh escaping me. "Aren't you beautiful?"

With a friendly touch, I ran my fingers along its strong neck, finding its mane, which was somehow softer and silkier than it looked and was like warm sand through my fingers. It nuzzled into me again and grunted quietly.

"Hey, Peter," I whispered over my shoulder. "The apple."

Peter was a few cautious feet behind. "This is something else, huh?" he said as he caught up.

"Yeah, can you believe this?"

I took the apple from Peter's hand, offering it slowly up to the creature. The unicorn sniffed at it but didn't bite.

"What? You don't like apples?" I asked, realizing with regret that we had left the carrots in the tent.

The unicorn sniffed once more at the apple, then followed a

scent down the length of my arm, stopping at my neck. It snuffled at my collar.

"What is it?" I asked, but then I realized.

I pulled the candy necklace Peter had given me out from under my shirt. The unicorn sniffed more fervently and began to chew on the heart pendant.

"Oh, you like that, do you?" I said with a laugh. I turned to Peter. "Sorry."

Peter shrugged and stood astonished as the unicorn continued to eat.

"Hey, careful. There's a string in there," I said to the unicorn, who kept on with the candy. I guided the necklace around as it munched happily, leaving only the elastic strand remaining around my neck.

It stopped chewing and we all stood and stared at each other with the stillness of the night, quiet all around us.

"Where did you come from?" I asked.

Its eyes stared into mine. It turned its neck and gazed at the forest behind it.

I glanced at the trail, then at Peter. "Do you think it lives in there?"

"I don't know," said a befuddled Peter.

We both glanced curiously toward the woods, then back to the unicorn.

"Do you live there?" I asked.

The unicorn turned again toward the dark forest, this time taking a step back. It repeated this, moving its head and pointing at the trees in a summoning motion.

"I think it wants us to follow it."

"Ellie, no. Your dad will kill us if we go out there," said Peter.

He was right. "I can't," I whispered to the creature. "I'm sorry."

It nodded at me. *Yes.* I was sure it had nodded.

"I think it understands me," I gasped.

The unicorn took a few steps back. I thought it was leaving, but it settled itself just a few feet away, keeping its gaze locked on mine.

It raised its head, stretching its neck high so its horn extended and reached to the sky above. A light flicked on at the tip of the horn, and a bright, glowing orb beamed out, painting a new guiding star in the sky.

The orb detached itself from the horn and floated freely above us. Higher and higher it rose. It brightened and radiated out, growing larger, and soon a fuzzy new moon hung in the sky, eclipsing our own.

"Ellie, what's going on?"

There was a tremble in Peter's voice. I too felt the hair on my arms prick, and the fear I had eluded before was now at my door, and it was pounding violently.

The light, hovering above us, stretched. It expanded out and curved down like the umbrella-shaped bell of a very large jellyfish, and before I knew it, it had formed a dome that encapsulated us on all sides. It pulsed and brightened. It was blinding.

Peter and I raised our hands to shield our ears as a high-pitched ringing dispensed from the surrounding light. The sound occupied and filled the dome, rising in intensity with each painful note and finally reaching a pitch just beyond our hearing.

The dome pulsed, and with one last rise in sound, the light

shattered and dispersed. And as if a power switch had been turned off, all was dark and quiet once more.

I looked to the unicorn—its eyes fixed on me. "What just happened?"

It lowered its head and nudged its big nose toward the house behind me.

"What?"

"Ellie," said Peter. "I think we should check the house."

The unicorn nodded.

"Why? What did you do?" I asked. "Did something happen to Dad? Are they okay?"

It pointed its nose to the house again.

Panic set in. *Dad! Millie!* That light. I didn't notice how far it stretched. Did it reach the house? What would happen if it did?

I looked at Peter, scared.

"I'll go see," he said.

He took off in a sprint. The back door slammed as he went inside. I waited.

It was taking too long. I took a step toward the house, intending to go in after him, but the back door creaked open again.

Peter stepped out. He slowly made his way back to me. So everything was fine then—Dad and Millie were okay. But as he walked, he came out from under the shadow of the big oak tree. And when he did, the moonlight fell on his face to reveal a look of utter terror.

"What!" I screamed.

"Th-the-they . . ." he stammered.

"What!"

I was about to make a dash for the house when someone answered me.

"They are fine!"

It wasn't Peter who spoke. The voice had come from the woods behind us.

Peter and I turned on our heels and stared toward the forest.

In the shadow of the trees, a dark figure stood.

16

"Who's there?" I called, my lips quivering with fear.

"You need not be afraid. I am a friend," the voice answered.

I glanced over at Peter, who was staring wide-eyed at me. I took a sideways step closer to him, and we stood with our knees shaking in unison as we stared into the darkness.

He emerged. At first, he was just a silhouette, a shadowy figure coming from the trees. Then he crossed into the moonlight and walked toward us.

The light lit a tall figure of a man. But as he strode closer, the glow of the moon washed over his strange features and I saw that he wasn't a man at all.

I marveled at the figure in white that stood before us.

He was slender and tall with skin so pale it was translucent. It was milky yet clear like steam trapped behind glass, and it stretched smoothly and youthfully over his face and sizable frame, making me think he was young, maybe just a few years older than me.

On his head, snow-white hair draped and fell in soft, straight lines, forming a wispy waterfall that cascaded down, framing his large doe-like eyes.

Around his neck glowed a lavender vial. A vest, white and leathery, draped over his shoulders and lay open at his bare chest. At his naval, his soft skin roughened into bumpy, iridescent scales that changed from a shimmery blue to a shimmery silver when he breathed. He continued the look of white, with long flowing trousers that looked silky and soft, and sticking out at the ends, his feet were bare in the icy snow.

He stopped beside the unicorn.

"Who are you?" I asked.

"Miss Cordelia Amora Heart, my deepest pleasure." The figure sank slowly to one knee in a low, poised bow. He rose again. "My name is Levvi," he said. "I am from the city of Glacia, your native land and home. I have come tonight to seek your help."

He waited for my response.

I stared at him blankly. His words had hit my ears in a jumbled mess that made no sense. "M-m-my help? L-land . . . of . . . Glacia?" I tripped.

"Yes, I implore you, with my utmost reverence and gratitude for your kindness, to take heed of my plea tonight. You and you alone hold the power and strength to save us. You are Glacia's last hope. I have been sent here to seek your help, so perhaps with you by our side, we can finally be free again."

I stared at him in silence. His words had left me dumbfounded, and an exasperated laugh escaped me.

"What are you talking about? Glacia? Where is that?" I glanced over at Peter, whose look of confusion confirmed that there were no towns or cities with that name anywhere close by. Dumbstruck, we both stared at the strange creature in front of us.

"It is my home. Yours, too, if you would have it."

"No," I said with nervous laughter. "You're mistaken."

"I am not mistaken, my princess. I am quite sure," he said. His eyes, peering into mine, were steady and sincere.

"What? I'm *not* a princess," I said. With these words, I was sure I felt the solid world on which my feet were planted begin to give way to sinking sand. I would soon be swallowed whole.

"Ah . . ." he said. "But you are."

He stared at me with big eyes that did not flinch.

I looked around, first to Peter, who stared back, wide-eyed and scared. Then to the magically beautiful unicorn, whose eyes locked with mine. Its gaze brought warmth and comfort, and I felt secure there. I then turned to the strange man who had come tonight to utter nonsense. Surely, it was all a dream.

He saw my disquiet, and a look of compassion shown on his face. "I cannot explain it all here," he said. "I do not think that would do. I must show you if you are to believe. Come with me now, before it is too late."

I shook my head. "I can't go anywhere with you. My dad will . . ." And then I remembered—*Dad!* I turned to Peter. "What was wrong with Dad? Are they okay?"

Levvi spoke before Peter could. "Your dad is fine. He has merely been paused."

"What?" I glared at him. My frustration with this night, and with this strange being, was starting to wear on me. "What did you do to my dad?"

"They were both frozen solid, like statues," whispered Peter.

"What?" I asked. I looked at Peter, confused, unsure if I'd heard him right.

"Everything was stopped, even the TV," he said.

I turned to Levvi, expecting an explanation.

"They are okay. They have been paused—that is all," he said.

"What do you mean?" I asked. "I don't understand."

"Midnight, here." He gestured to the unicorn. "He has slowed time for them. Have no fear. They have no need to worry now."

"What?" Again, his words baffled me. "Do you mean to say you stopped time?" I asked. Sand shifted at my feet.

"Not exactly." He laughed. "Time is constant. It cannot be stopped or started. We are now merely synced with the flow of our time in Glacia. To us, your father may seem 'frozen' or 'paused,' but I assure you nothing has changed for him. He is experiencing time as he always has. Though we perceive him as moving slower, it is in fact we who are moving faster. However, I suppose you can look at it either way. Time in Glacia moves much faster than it does here. We are now existing at a speed that is thousands of times faster than that of your own."

"And what does that mean exactly?" I asked, because it was all too much for my mind to process.

"It means your dad is still sitting and watching his movie in the living room. He may have just noticed a quick blur in front of his eyes when Peter, here, waved his hands in his face, but it was only a split-second's time, and he is likely to give it no thought at all."

"How do you know what happened in the house?" I asked.

"How do you know my name?" asked Peter.

"We are quite telepathic and can read untrained minds," he said. "Peter, you are an open book to me. You, Princess Cordelia"—he stopped and looked at Peter thoughtfully—"or *Ellie*, as Peter would call you, are closed." He smiled at me. "But that does not surprise me, knowing who your grandmother was and all."

"My grandmother? How do you know my grandmother?"

"Ah, all in good time, my princess. I will explain. But we must go now."

17

I stood, chewing on my lip and staring at the two strange creatures that were waiting by the forest's edge.

I turned to Peter. "Come on, Peter. Please."

"Do you really think this is a good idea?" he asked. He looked past me to Levvi and Midnight. "For all we know, they could be leading us into a trap."

I swayed back and forth, thinking. "I know, but . . ."

What was I going to say? He was right. It was crazy. But how could I let something like this go? It was all too strange and too puzzling to just leave it. My curiosity wasn't going to allow for that. "Please," I begged.

"But, Ellie . . ." His eyes were pleading back.

"You don't have to go, Peter," I said. "It's okay."

He looked at me, disturbed. "You're kidding, right? You can't go alone."

I felt my patience waning. I breathed a heavy sigh because it was more than just impatience, more than curiosity. There was something gripping my heart, pulling on me—and it wasn't giving. "I gotta go, Peter," I muttered, succumbing to the relentless strain.

Peter stared at me with defeated eyes. "Okay," he said, but his tone told me he was still rejecting the idea. He glanced toward the forest again, then back to me. "Okay," he repeated, still sounding torn. "I'll go." He shook his head. "It's stupid, but . . . I'll go."

We trailed a good distance behind the two strange creatures, both of us probably thinking the same foolish thing—that if we needed to run, we would at least have a head start.

Midnight lit the way with his magical light, so bright and beautiful on the tip of his spiral horn. It was a strange, slow walk that was like a weird dream. The night air around us was oddly tepid and eerily quiet—no wind, no leaves, no howl of a coyote in the distance. There was only the faint muffled sound of our footsteps on what should have been loud, crunchy snow and sticks.

I slipped an arm into Peter's beside me.

"You okay?" he whispered.

"Yeah," I said, feeling like a guilty fool. Now that we were actually going, I was starting to see how tremendously stupid it was—and dragging Peter with me was the worst of it. If anything were to happen to him . . .

I took a shaky breath and tried to push down the fears, but they settled somewhere deep and started to ache.

We came to the end of the trail, where it opened up to the lake. Levvi and Midnight, still a good distance ahead, stopped and waited for Peter and me to catch up. We walked to stand beside their large, peculiar forms, and suddenly I felt very small and frail. A nervous shiver ran through me.

Levvi met my gaze with concern in his eyes. "We are nearly there," he said. "Follow me and do not be afraid." His words did nothing to ease my mind and only worked to renew my fears, as I imagined it was the same thing he would say regardless of his intentions.

Levvi and Midnight stepped off the trail and started toward the lake.

I hesitated, a sick worry trickling over my skin. It was as though I was on the edge of something, about to cross over. I whispered a prayer and hoped there would be a bridge and not just a towering precipice to walk over.

I might have turned back here, for my legs started to shake and my nerves moved my teeth in a noisy chatter, but Peter took the first step, and I followed.

We were on the beach. Levvi and Midnight sauntered toward the icy lake. Without hesitation, they crossed the foreshore and walked on top of the frozen water.

Peter and I paused at the edge. It was now spring, and the days had begun to warm enough for us to know it would be unsafe.

We both looked on as Levvi and Midnight gained in distance. The heavy beast stepped across the ice, but it did not crack. Levvi turned back and saw that we had not moved beyond the shore.

"You will be fine," he called out to us. "The ice will hold. Remember, the world around us is frozen. You will have moved past any weak points before the molecules have time to react. You are a weightless bird out here tonight." He scooped the air with a big outstretched hand, gesturing for us to follow. "Now, make haste. We have not got all night."

I hesitated, and Peter took the first step again. He turned back when he noticed I wasn't moving. "You okay?" he asked.

"I don't know, Peter," I said. "Maybe you were right. This is a little crazy, huh?"

Peter pressed his lips together, looking unsure. "I think it's going to be okay. We gotta see, right?"

He smiled warmly, and I could tell he was trying to be brave for me.

"Yeah," I said.

He held out his hand, and I tentatively stepped forward.

Peter guided me to the spot where Levvi and Midnight had stopped beside a large boulder peeking out from the frozen water.

The ice held.

"Now that we are all here," said Levvi. "It's time to go home."

"You live in the lake?" I said, panic setting in. How would that work? How would we breathe?

"No," he said.

I breathed a sigh of relief.

"We live *under* the lake," he said with a smile. "Now, Midnight!"

Midnight acted on his command, lowering his horn to the ice. The tip brightened, and light radiated out, drawing a large circle around us. There was a loud buzzing noise and then a whirl of high notes that accompanied the circling light as it dazzled and danced on the surface of the lake.

With a loud *whoosh*, we were falling.

Like a laser, the light had cut a large slab in the ice. It was now a floor under our feet, and a sheer wall of ice rose around us as we fell.

We descended rapidly, like a snapped elevator, and the icy walls changed to a murky wall of lake water that held firm at the sides and miraculously did not spill in and flood us.

The elevator continued down, and the water changed to rocks and dirt, then to ice again. But to my amazement, it wasn't ice at all.

A bright light danced and bounced off the crystalline surface, creating shimmery sparkles. They were not walls made of ice but were a solid crystal that shifted from an opaque white to a sparkly clear diamond as we moved.

Dazzling rainbows bounced and beamed around us. I looked at Peter, who gazed around, mesmerized by the scene. His eyes fell on mine and we stared at each other, wide-eyed and grinning, as the rainbows played across our faces.

The elevator stopped.

"We are here," said Levvi.

He pressed an invisible button on the wall. It lit a circle around his finger, and a solid stone door in front of us turned to vapor.

We stepped out of the elevator and my jaw dropped.

The room we had entered was enormous—a spectacularly large cavern cut from stone. Its floors and walls were composed of the same white crystal as the elevator, and it stretched out far and wide, covering the room in a blanket of sparkling white.

I stared in awe.

The room was bustling with activity. Creatures that resembled Levvi, with their pasty pale skin, filled the space. Unlike Levvi, though, many of these figures had hair in a rainbow of breathtaking colors.

Among the strange figures, dressed in white, were several white unicorns just as beautiful and poised as Midnight—all with an array of pastel rainbows coloring their manes and tails.

The chattering noise from the crowd bounced off the walls of the large room, creating an echo of ambient sound that reminded me of the busy train station in the city.

There were several pools of sparkling blue water casually

scattered throughout the grounds, with white crystal bridges and pathways winding around and stretching over the pools. Pops of vibrant-colored hair in various shades of reds, blues, and pinks moved throughout the waters as figures swam.

High on the ceiling above, so magnificently far up that I felt like I would fall over if I were to continue to crane my neck in that direction, was a large domed skylight. It shined a bright light down into the white room, illuminating the entire space brilliantly.

To my right was a smaller space separate from the main room. Its walls were scooped and curved, creating a cozy enclosure, like a large den ready and awaiting a giant, sleepy bear. There was a roaring fireplace situated on the back wall of the den, and a round, steaming pool was off to the side, with several folks lazily relaxing in the mist.

At the far end of the main room, a towering wall rose as high as a cliff. It homed a breathtaking array of rough-cut, crystal clusters that jutted out at various intervals, displaying many beautifully cut facets that shimmered and sparkled along its surface.

In the mid-center of the wall fell a curtain of water that streamed around and over a stone arched opening. Steamy bubbles cascaded down on both sides where they fell and hit the stone floor with a splash.

And to my utter astonishment—and complete disbelief—the remaining wall to my left was a clear, blue, sparkling panel of water, smooth and still like a fishbowl. However, there was no glass. And a young boy, walking hand in hand with his mother, stretched out playful fingers to glide them along the smooth surface. His fingers rippled through with ease, and a stream of water splashed down, creating puddles at his feet.

The tranquil sea outside was a luminous blue world of water. Hundreds of shimmery fish swam in and out of a system of spectacularly colored coral reefs. The reef rose in layers from the white sandy seabed, creating a garden that bloomed in a vivid display of colors.

The rocky life teamed with creatures I didn't recognize. A school of funny-looking pink, balloon-shaped fish weaved in and out of vibrant green kelp. A dozen jellyfish-like creatures with glowing rainbow tentacles lazily bobbed along near the surface of the wall. The jellyfish were followed by a large tangerine manta ray with a watchful cycloptic eye. It swooped down along the wall, leaving a cascade of bubbles in its wake.

And then I noticed them. The brightly colored pops of hair that had been swimming in the pools were also swimming around outside.

There was a small group of individuals clustered together in a tight circle, and in a beautifully synchronized burst, they pushed off and out from one another like a flowering fireworks display, revealing a dozen shimmery fish tails that gracefully fluttered in the water.

A pretty young girl, who broke from the group, swam down the length of the wall to a large arch made of white stone. It acted as a sort of door connecting the two spaces, and she swam down and through the opening, where she was poured out into a stream. The stream carved its way into the stony floor of the main room.

She swam until reaching a stone ledge and pulled herself up. She lifted a metallic green and violet tail from the water. Droplets spilled and splashed off the ends of her tail fins. In an instant, the tail faded into legs that were now covered in a shimmery white skirt.

"You're mermaids!" I exclaimed.

I looked at Levvi unbelievingly and then to Peter, who stared slack-jawed at the scene before us.

"Yes," said Levvi with a smile. "Though some of us prefer mermen."

I laughed. "Levvi, this is wonderful!"

I gazed around in amazement. The sheer beauty of it all was overwhelming, and my eyes brimmed with tears.

"I am glad you like it, my princess, for it is your home."

I shook my head in disbelief.

He held out his hand to me. "Come with me. I will show you more."

I took Levvi's hand as he guided me through the room. Midnight and Peter followed closely behind.

"This, my princess," he said, "is the main center of our city, Glacia."

He lifted stretched arms and swept them proudly around the room. My eyes followed his fingers, and the magnitude of the beauty before me hit me once again. I stared, amazed.

He led us down a stone path that followed along the edge of one of the pools. It circled around, and we came to stand beside the unbridled wall of water. I marveled as I watched a young mermaid playing outside in the blue abyss—so happy and free, swimming in the water with her beautiful green tail.

"This here is the main entrance," said Levvi. He pointed to the arched door I had seen the mermaid swim through before.

I looked through the arch opening out into the beautiful sea. The water moved and flowed through a channel, and I was amazed to see it didn't all spill in and flood the place. I shuddered to think what would happen if it did.

"Farther down," continued Levvi, "through that arched door in the back, are miles of passages that lead to the rest of the city. That is where you will also find the private quarters of our citizens."

"Is this where *all* mermaids live?" I asked.

"Oh, no." He laughed. "Not quite. We are just one city, though we are a large one. Many merfolk live in smaller groups apart from us and they are scattered all over your world."

"So you've always lived here? Below us?" asked Peter.

"Yes, Glacia is an ancient city. We were here even before humans walked the land above."

I stared, bewildered. "So all the legends are true?"

He laughed again. "Oh, no. I am sure they are not, but I suspect many have origins based in reality."

"What about Midnight?" I asked. "Do unicorns also live here?"

"They do not live here. Not really. Some have found a home here, but mostly they are land creatures."

"So where do they live?" asked Peter.

"They live in the forest," said Levvi.

"What forest?" Peter's face lit with excitement.

"Yes," said Levvi, leaving me and Peter to stare at each other in confusion.

"Huh?" we said together.

"Oh, I am sorry. I was responding to the question you asked in your mind," said Levvi. "They do live in your forest above, and yes, they are the ones who have formed the magnificent trails you walk.

They make their homes in forests all over the world, though they are more adaptive to colder regions."

"But how come we've never seen them?" asked Peter.

"That is because their magic conceals them and allows them to move as ghosts through your world," said Levvi.

"Is that the same magic that keeps everybody away from the lake?" I asked. I was sure now that that was it.

Levvi's eyes brightened. "Oh, well, we merfolk have our own magic for that," he said with a wink. "But now, I am sorry. We must move on. Perhaps we can arrange another visit soon and I can give you a proper tour and answer all your questions at that time. Follow me."

Peter and I followed Levvi as he and Midnight guided us through the crowd. Many eyes looked our way, and Levvi greeted each with a friendly nod as we passed.

As we walked, we crossed over a delicately carved stone footbridge. The water below was as clear as diamonds, and a single small blue fish swam around in circles beneath us.

We came to the back of the room, where the stone wall towered high above, and we passed under the archway in the middle.

The noise from the raining waterfall echoed into a long, dark hallway that extended out in front of us. Midnight's horn beamed brightly, and we followed him and Levvi down the lengthy passageway.

To my right, several archways opened up into more tunnels, which Levvi pointed out were the entrances that led to the sleeping quarters, the pasture for the unicorns, the queen's chamber, the dining hall, and other various locations in the city.

We continued down for some time before walking through another door at the end. Here the floor slanted up, turning into a ramp. The slanted floor curved up and around, running along the wall of the circular room like a spiral staircase. A stone rail ran along the inner edge. I rested my hand on it and stopped.

"Peter," I said, calling him over. He had just entered through the door behind me. "Look!" I pointed over the rail.

He peered out, and we both stood with our heads leaning over the rail, looking up and then down again in amazement. The serpentine floor wound beautifully in a concentric spiral that towered up for hundreds of feet above us. Peter stepped back.

"That makes me a little dizzy," he said.

"Yeah," I agreed. "Oh, look, we gotta get going."

I pointed at Levvi and Midnight, who had continued to walk and were now higher up on the other side of the tubular space, directly across from us. Peter and I ran to catch up.

We walked for some time, climbing higher with each step. At last, we exited through a door on the side. We entered a narrow hallway and followed it down until we came to another room at the end.

19

This room was much smaller than the entrance hall. It was dome-shaped, like a carved stone bowl flipped upside down. The walls were marked with several cut-out windows running along the length of them, each one with a curtain of water splashing down behind.

At the top and in the center of the dome, there was a prismed sunroof with a bright light shining through. The dazzling light cast hundreds of colorful rainbows around the room, and they bounced off the water of a large round pool centered on the ground below.

The pool was filled with dozens of merfolk swimming around and hanging off the edge as they chatted. They were speaking in a strange, melodious language that came very close to something that sounded like singing, and it echoed a lovely song around the stony room. Levvi led us over to the group.

One by one, as they saw us, the mermen and merwomen pulled their fins from the water and hopped out of the pool on legs. There was a chorus of voices as each of the individuals stretched out their hands to greet us. Their smiling faces were warm and friendly, but the fervent attention was daunting and working to set me on edge.

Levvi motioned Peter and me over to a stone bench that circled the perimeter of the pool. I found a spot on the bench and sat down. Peter followed, sitting with shaky legs beside me.

"Good evening, my friends," said Levvi to the group.

The merfolk quieted down, some settling into the pool with their soft fluttering tails, with a dozen more finding their seats on the stone bench beside us.

"I welcome you," said Levvi. "But we must be quick tonight. Our guests are from the land above and are borrowing our time. And to avoid any confusion, let us also remember to keep to their language tonight."

Levvi motioned for me to stand. I followed his orders on weak knees.

"May I introduce to you Miss Cordelia Amora Heart," he said. He smiled at me and added, "Our princess!"

The crowd cheered, and applause filled the air. Every face was a spotlight upon me, and my knees quivered. I sat back down next to Peter, feeling uneasy. He found my hand beside him and kept it firmly in his.

Levvi waited patiently for the crowd to quiet.

"She has joined me tonight on a single strand of faith, and I promised we would provide answers and the information she needs to decide," he said. He turned and spoke to a pretty mermaid who sat across the circle from us. "Starla, will you so kindly give Princess Cordelia a brief summary of her connection and history to Glacia?"

Starla looked cheerfully at me. She had shiny magenta hair that draped smoothly over her pale shoulders. A pointy pink nose and rosy cheeks matched her hair. She wore a strappy, white pearled top that stopped just at her naval. And in place of her tail was a long flowing skirt in a shimmery white. She was lovely.

"Yes, Levvi," said Starla. She turned to me. "Oh, Cordelia, my sweet and beautiful princess, it is my greatest pleasure to meet you—"

"Quickly, if we could, Starla," interrupted Levvi.

"Yes, of course," said Starla. She stared down at her lap and continued, this time reading from a stone tablet in her hands. "Cordelia Amora Heart, it is my greatest pleasure." She smiled at me. "I am here to inform you that you are the descendant of the most high and admirable Queen Zera, who ruled our city with love and honor for many years.

"Queen Zera was the loveliest and kindest of rulers, and as a nation, we flourished and prospered during her reign, so much so that much of what you see today in Glacia is a direct result of the Golden Age of Zera. She remained in power until the end of her long life, whereupon her great-granddaughter, Leira, took up the throne.

"Leira was a kind and lovely ruler, but her time as our leader was cut short, for she was young, and her heart betrayed us when she fell in love with a human. She abandoned us for him and for a life in the world above.

"Without our queen, we were left vulnerable and scared. We carried on the best we could, managing a peaceful and happy life, even though we were without a queen and the protection of her magic.

"But we did not know that amongst us—disguised as a friend

and fellow mermaid—there lurked an evil witch. And while we were naively living our peaceful lives, her darkness brewed and bubbled.

"Razora was a witty and cunningly clever mermaid, and she was the best friend who Leira left behind. But we are sure not even Leira knew of the corruption in her heart.

"And once Leira, her only friend, was gone, Razora had no reason to carry on pretending for the rest of us.

"When we finally saw her true colors, it was already too late.

"And when we realized her heart's true intentions, ours broke.

"Razora desired to be queen. We thought it should have been impossible, for the queen's magic is transferable only to the rightful heiress. But she was somehow able to bypass that ancient and deeply set law, and she obtained the power of the queen.

"Unlike the sweet and pure magic of the true queen, Razora's magic was dark and bitter, and it brought destruction to our lovely city.

"A dark shadow was cast over us as she sat as queen, and those cold, dark days are remembered with fear and sadness. We lost so much and many poor souls to her evil ways.

"But graciously, those dreadful days did not last long, for one morning, we woke to discover Razora was gone.

"And we have gone on now for many years believing she had passed and her threat had been buried with her, but once again, we were wrong.

"She is back . . . and she is again hovering over us, threatening to take over and destroy Glacia and the beautiful merpeople that live here.

"We are weak against her because she is still queen. A queen's power surpasses any other, and only the true heiress would have the power to fight against Razora.

"We need our princess to take the throne, giving Razora no power over us anymore.

"Once the heiress returns and we have our true queen, Razora will be powerless and we will be released from her chains for good.

"You, my dear, are that said heiress. And our hope is that you may consider helping us."

Starla finished and looked up from the stone tablet.

I tried to swallow the magnitude of what she had just spewed at me, but my throat was so scratchy and dry. I coughed a dry cough and scanned the room. So many hopeful, pleading, sad eyes stared right at me. I met them with sorrow and pity.

I chewed my lip and sighed. Obviously, there had been a mistake.

"I don't know what to say," I said. "I'm sorry, but I'm not who you think I am."

A large merman who sat beside Starla spoke. "Levvi," he said. "Did you not get the right child?"

Levvi looked at me with an affectionate smile. "It is she," he said. "But she was never informed of any of this until tonight."

"But surely your great-grandmother has told you about us?" asked the same merman again.

I sighed. And then I laughed. And then I sighed again. "My grandmother? Who?" I asked with another laugh. "Do you mean Granny Leira? I didn't even know her," I said, raising my hands, trying to show them this wasn't my burden. "I can't help you guys."

"But you must," said the large merman. "You are the heiress."

I shook my head at him but decided to play along. "So if I'm the heiress . . . doesn't that mean my mom was, too? Why didn't you guys contact her or her father before her?"

"Leira's son, your mother's father, would not have been able to rule in Glacia as it is only queens who possess the magic. And yes, your mother would have been the next in line," answered Starla. "We do not know the circumstances leading to it, but she was given up for adoption when she was still a baby. We could not locate her after that, and Razora seemed to have relented by that time, so we did not try. It was just recently, when Razora came back out of hiding, that we sought Queen Leira's help."

"So Granny Leira told you where I was?"

"She brought you to us," said Starla.

I laughed, but I wanted to cry. The house—from my lovely, kind grandmother—had just been a ploy. I glanced at Peter, who was staring at the crowd with narrowed eyes.

I turned back to them. "And what about Granny Leira?" I asked. "How come she didn't help you herself? Couldn't she have just killed Razora or something?"

Starla spoke solemnly. "Queen Leira was very old and frail by the time Razora reemerged. Your grandmother's time with us was short after that. We think Razora may have waited so long for just that reason."

"And Leira still loved and remembered her friend from the past," said Levvi. "She refused to come against her."

"What about before? Back when Razora was ruling as queen here. Granny Leira wouldn't have been so old. Couldn't she have come back as queen?"

Levvi spoke again. "The world above was closed to us during Razora's rule. Because of this, Leira was unaware of our troubles with her at that time." Levvi paused. "We are not sure she would have chosen us over her life above, anyway."

"So what exactly do you want from me?" I asked, completely exasperated. "Are you asking me to kill her?"

Levvi shook his head. "It would not need to come to that," he said. "With you here as queen, her powers would fade."

I laughed. "But I'm just a kid. I can't rule a city."

"It is your destiny," said a long-faced merman looking at me crossly.

"What about my life?"

"The magic is in you," said the merman again. "Without you, our world will crumble under Razora's control."

There was silence as they waited for me to answer him. I stared into the many sad eyes staring so hopelessly at me. I didn't know what to say, but a strange burden started to weigh on me, and the pressure to say or do something to help ease their pain was straining my heart.

I continued to stare in silence, not knowing what to do.

Then a quiet voice spoke beside me. "You don't need her."

It was Peter.

The room turned to look at him. They each donned the same expression of puzzlement; it seemed they were noticing his presence for the first time.

"I mean," he continued timidly, "there must be something you're missing. You say only the rightful heir can be queen, but that didn't stop Razora. What's up with that?" he asked.

Bewildered eyes fell upon him, and the room was quiet.

"We do not fully understand it," answered Levvi, breaking the silence. "We continue to pore over the laws, searching for answers, but we have not yet found anything that will solve this riddle."

"I think Ellie and I should read the law for ourselves," said Peter.

The many eyes glaring at Peter turned from bewildered to disapproving.

"Who are you, boy?" asked a merwoman sitting on the edge of the pool.

"I'm a friend," he answered.

"Well, friend," she said with an air of condescension I didn't very well like. "Perhaps you should leave these matters to those whom they concern."

"That's right," another merman echoed in agreement.

More merfolk began to pipe up, throwing their callous disapprovals at Peter. He sank back on the bench, looking scared. Their blatant disregard for him was all I needed to see.

"I won't do this for you," I said, pulling their angry eyes from Peter's and back to mine. I held their gaze.

An uproar ensued among the merfolk, and Levvi and Starla exchanged a look of frustration directed toward the angry crowd.

"Quiet! Quiet everyone!" shouted Levvi.

It took a moment for the group to calm. They turned disgruntled faces in Levvi's direction.

"How could this come as a surprise to any of you?" he asked through pursed lips. "We have gone over this hundreds of times, knowing full well this was likely to be the answer."

"But we need her!" a voice demanded.

"Yes, perhaps we do. But she does not need us."

Levvi turned to me and then to Peter with a kind smile. "We are asking the world of her, quite literally. Perhaps we could do a little more than treat her best friend as an outcast."

Levvi's eyes fell to his feet and he was quiet. His sad, forlorn expression broke my heart. I turned to Starla, who met me with kind eyes, and I glanced around the room at some of the individuals who had remained quiet during the uproar.

"Do you have anything to say?" I asked. My gaze was directed at a young mermaid who was sitting opposite us on the bench.

She glanced up timidly and rose from her seat. She spoke in a hushed voice. "Please forgive us, Princess. We are just scared. Fear does not suit us well, as you can see." She bowed gracefully and sat back down.

I glanced around the room at the poor souls in front of me. They didn't look so angry anymore; they just looked scared and sad.

"I'm sorry, but I can't do this," I said. "I'm just a girl. I am not this princess you are talking about—even if it's true that I'm the heiress."

Unexpected tears fell from my eyes as my words hit each of them like tiny daggers to their hearts. With sunken shoulders and forlorn eyes, they were now quiet.

"It is okay, my princess," said Levvi. "But would you perhaps think on it a little more?" His voice was dry and crumpled with despair, and it broke my heart.

"Okay," I said. "I can do that."

My answer came as a surprise to both of us.

Levvi met my gaze with gratitude. "Thank you," he said, and

there was a resounding echo of thanks around the room. "Then we will leave it at that. And we will wait for Princess Cordelia to decide in her time. Now, she must be heading back."

"I will not come again," said Levvi. "It is up to you to decide. We will wait and accept your decision, whatever it may be."

We stood on top of the frozen lake. The night sky above twinkled with millions of stars, and the bright moon beamed upon us. I ran my fingers through Midnight's warm mane and stared into his big eyes, thinking.

"How much time do I have?"

Levvi smiled. "The sooner, the better, since your time here will move the days along for us very quickly. But we can wait for our princess. Razora will have to yield to you . . . whenever it is you decide to come."

"Where is she now?"

"She is hiding for now, but she emerges as she pleases, to threaten and attack."

"She is toying with you?" I asked. "Why? Why not just take over now?"

"I do not know her reasons for any of it," said Levvi. "But I do know from the stories of my father and his father before that she only ever desired to destroy. We must assume that is still her plan."

"Destroy Glacia?" I sighed. "I can't even imagine. It's so beautiful."

"It is," said Levvi with a smile.

"How would I get back?" I asked.

"Use your locket," said Levvi, smiling even bigger now.

"My locket?"

"Yes, it is the key to the gateway here at the lake. Leira told me she would leave it for you. Did she not?"

"You mean the heart locket from my closet?"

"Yes, I am sure that would be it," he said. "Take it with you and lower it into the water near this boulder here. The same as Midnight did with his horn. It will start the descent."

Levvi then smiled at me. It was warm and kind, and I knew at that moment he was a friend.

He took my hand in his. "And now," he said, "it is time for me to part. You, Cordel—"

"Call me Ellie."

He nodded. "You, Ellie, are the princess I knew you would be, and I am very glad to have met you tonight." He bowed low and kissed my hand. "Midnight will lead you the rest of the way home. Farewell, my princess, and you too, Peter. I hope to see you both again soon."

"Bye," I said.

Levvi started to go. He stopped, turning back to me. "Ellie," he said. "Did you like your room?"

"My room?"

"Leira asked us to tend to the house once she was gone. Starla is the one who decorated the attic."

"Yes," I said with a smile. "Tell her I love it."

"Very well," he said and returned to the lake.

At the edge of the yard, Midnight lowered his horn and a burst of light whizzed around us. In an instant, Peter and I were back in our time with the cold, biting air on our skin and the wind rustling the trees in the dark night.

We said goodbye to the magical creature and made our way back to the porch. We had just settled ourselves back in the tent when the back door creaked open.

"You guys all right out there?" called Dad.

My heart stopped. *Oh crap.* I needed to sound normal. "Yep, Dad, we're good," I said, feeling my nerves rattle in my throat and thinking I had given something away.

"Spot any unicorns yet?" badgered an unsuspecting Dad.

I looked at Peter, smiling big. I called back to Dad, "Nope. No luck." Peter and I started to laugh. "I think you were right, Dad. It was just a deer."

20

I was staring out the window when Mr. McNeil handed me my math test. He placed it on my desk upside down, which I knew couldn't be good. He looked at me sternly. "Got to stop daydreaming, Ellie," he chided before moving down the row.

I turned the paper over and scowled at the big fat F written obnoxiously in the brightest red ink I'd ever seen. As if the F for *fail* wasn't enough to drive the guilt home. I mean, did it seriously need to be so bright? I shoved the paper into my backpack. Yes, it was the first F I'd ever received in my life. No, I wasn't going to worry about it right now. I stared back out the window, waiting for the bell to ring.

School was the least of my worries at the moment, and trying to focus on it or care about it would be impossible, even if I wanted to. I was finding it hard to care about anything. We had been back from Glacia for a few days, but I hadn't been able to shake the strange night from my mind.

To be honest, I was feeling very lost. Completely and utterly lost, like someone had picked me up, blindfolded me, then tossed me at some random spot in the galaxy—lost.

I wasn't coping too well with my ginormous new world. It was just so huge. So much. What was the proper protocol for dealing with something like this, anyway? I was sure I was getting it all wrong. My world had expanded substantially, to say the least, but instead of growing with it, I felt like I was being stretched and pulled in order to fit.

And the craziest part was that I wanted to. I wanted to fit. I couldn't just let Glacia go like Peter had told me to do when he left on Sunday. He thought we should just forget about it. That it wasn't our problem. I wasn't having such an easy time letting it go like he was.

It felt like a big piece of my heart got stuck there, and I kept thinking about the strange world with a worry and longing I couldn't shake. It left me feeling unsettled, and I hadn't been sleeping well, eating well, or doing *anything* well, for that matter, since our return.

With the ring of the bell, I shuffled out of math class and headed toward the bathroom. The waft of oniony air moving through the halls worked to churn my already achy and worried stomach, and I was in no hurry to get to lunch.

I peed and flushed and opened the stall to find Bethany at the sink. She was standing at the mirror, repositioning the heap of curls on top of her head.

"Hey, Bethany," I said, walking over to wash my hands.

"Oh hey, Ellie," she said. She had an elastic band in her mouth and was smoothing out the top of her hair.

"You should wear it down."

She glowered at me through the mirror. "This mess?"

"You've got gorgeous hair," I said, turning on the faucet. "I'm jealous." I frowned at my own drab, flat hair next to hers.

"Thanks," she said, letting her bouncy curls fall to her shoulders. She combed her fingers through them and scrunched up the ends, sulking at her reflection. "Eh, not today." She hurriedly pulled her hair back up.

"Sorry about the other day," I said, grabbing at some paper towels and turning to Bethany.

"So you're really going out with Peter Evans?" she asked. She finished twisting the elastic around her hair, then pulled a tube of lip gloss from her backpack. She moved the wand over her lips and smacked them in the mirror.

"No, not really," I said, feeling stupid now for saying that. "We're just friends."

Bethany turned away from the mirror to look at me. "How'd that happen?"

I shrugged. "Just kind of happened. He's cool, though. Maybe we can hang out sometime, so you guys can get to know him."

She laughed.

"What?" I asked, immediately finding my patience break.

"Oh, nothing," she said quickly, turning back to herself in the mirror. "Sure, maybe sometime."

I huffed at Bethany. She was still smirking a little, and the blood in my veins was heating uncomfortably. I shook my head, deciding to drop it. What did I care what she had to say about Peter, anyway?

"I suppose Jenny told you Alex dumped me?" she said, wisely changing the subject.

"Yeah," I said. "I'm so sorry."

"Yeah right. You're not sorry." I saw the roll of her eyes in the mirror.

"I'm sorry you got hurt," I said. "Are you okay?"

"I'm fine," she said. "It turns out you were right about him. It should have been me that dumped his sorry ass. You know he cheated on me?"

"Oh, really? I'm sorry."

"Yeah well," she said, patting her hair again. "His loss."

"Yeah," I agreed with a smile. "You're gonna find someone so much better than him, Bethany. You'll see."

She smiled but shrugged. "I'll have to go somewhere else to find him. This town is seriously dried up. I guess you figured that out pretty quickly," she said with a raised eyebrow.

"What do you mean?"

"Come on, Ellie. You and Peter? I mean, you can obviously do better than Peter Evans."

"What do you have against Peter?"

"I don't have anything against him. I'm just sayin'."

"Well, don't," I snapped. "I don't want to hear it."

"All right, gawd. I'll leave it," she said, putting her hands up in surrender. She turned to the door to leave, then called back to me, "Are you coming?"

21

There was a knock at the door.

"If you're Peter and not a robber, come in!" I shouted.

The door opened behind me. "That's not a great way to deter robbers," said Peter as he entered the kitchen.

I glanced over my shoulder at him. "Hi," I said.

He walked over and grabbed a stool beside me. "Apple crisp!" he exclaimed.

The dessert was bubbling and hot on the center island in front of us.

"Yeah," I said, smiling at him. "That's all yours, too. I just pulled it out. Grab some." I pointed my floury fingers at the plate and spoon I had set out for him.

"Are you making a pie, too?" he asked.

I shrugged. "Trying to distract myself. It's not really helping much."

"From what?" asked Peter. He shoved a spoonful of apple crisp into his mouth. "Ah, man." He closed his eyes and savored the bite. "From what?" he repeated, opening his eyes to look at me.

I shrugged again and looked down. I continued rolling out my pie crust.

He leaned into me. "Glacia, huh?" he whispered, not knowing where Dad or Millie was.

"Millie's taking a nap," I informed him.

"That was pretty crazy, huh?" said Peter, staring at his spoon in thought.

"Yeah," I agreed with a head bob. "Hey, there's ice cream in the freezer."

"Ah, man, Ellie. You got to stop," he said, moving off his stool. "I'm totally spoiled."

I laughed at him, then stared pensively at my messy fingers. "I can't stop thinking about it."

He scooped some ice cream onto his plate. "Yeah, me too."

"I'm thinking of going back."

Peter stuck the spoon in the ice cream and eyed me solemnly. "You're not serious, right?"

I flipped my dough and pressed on the roller. "I don't know." I swayed my head a little in thought and landed on Peter's worried eyes. I sighed. "I've just been feeling really weird since we got back."

I rolled the dough up over the rolling pin and then carefully back out over the pie.

"It was weird," agreed Peter. "Life-altering weird."

"Life-exploding for me," I said bleakly.

Peter eyed me thoughtfully. "Yeah, I bet." He put his hand on my shoulder and met my gaze. "But we don't need to go back, right?"

I stared back down at the ice cream, all beady and wet on the counter. I huffed a little and picked it up. I scooped another spoon out for Peter and put the lid back on, then put it away in the fridge.

"You okay?" asked Peter, standing rigid where I left him.

"Yeah," I said with a weak smile. "I'm fine." I went back to fiddling with my pie crust.

Peter leaned sideways into me, bumping my shoulder. "Here taste this," he said, holding up a spoon of apple crisp to me. "It'll make you feel better."

I took the bite compliantly.

"Did it help?"

I smiled at him. "Yeah," I said. "Short-lived, but yeah."

"Why don't we do something to get your mind off of things?" he suggested.

"Yeah, okay," I said. "Can we go to your house?" He still hadn't let me meet his mom, but the nerve-wracking scene of meeting her for the first time seemed like the perfect distraction to me.

Peter slumped. "I don't want to go there."

I finished crimping my pie and frowned at him. "Come on," I petitioned. "Your mom's going to start thinking I'm imaginary."

"She already does," he said with a laugh. He thought for a second and shook his head. "Not today. She's too stressed out. She didn't even want *me* there."

"What's she so stressed about?"

"Money," he said with a sigh. "Like always. She wants to go back to nursing school so she can get a better job, but that takes money she doesn't have."

"That sucks," I said. I put my pie in the fridge. "Puts my problems into perspective, I guess."

Peter smiled. "There you go."

"Do you want to go hang out at the lake?" I asked.

"Is that a good idea?"

"Why wouldn't it be?"

Peter shrugged. "I was thinking something to distract you from Glacia, not remind you of it."

I rolled my eyes a little. "It's the lake, Peter. I'll be fine."

Peter scrunched up his cheek, looking unsure. I saw the struggle on his face. He was obviously debating on whether or not it was worth arguing about. He folded with a sigh and smiled at me. "Let's go," he said.

"What are you thinking about?" asked Peter.

"Huh?"

"You're thinking about something," he said. He reached over and patted my head. I looked up from the trail to him.

"Oh, nothing," I said, realizing we'd made it all the way back home without a word between us. "These trails kind of hypnotize me."

"You've been quiet all day," he said. "What's up?"

I stopped and turned to him but focused my attention on some new baby buds forming on the branches near his shoulder instead.

He had been right. The lake was a bad idea. Instead of getting my mind off of things, it did exactly the opposite, and I had spent all afternoon thinking about the one thing I had meant to distract myself from.

"What?" he asked after a moment of me just staring into the thickets.

I moved my eyes to his and took a nervous breath. "I want to go back," I said.

He narrowed his gaze but didn't say anything.

"I know you think I shouldn't, but I want to."

"Ellie." He sighed. "I really think it's a bad idea."

"Why?" I asked. "Why is it so bad to want to help them?"

Peter studied me with troubled eyes. "Because . . . we don't know what could happen there. We don't know what that evil queen Razora wants. What if she tries to hurt you?"

"I don't think she can hurt me," I said weakly.

"You believe that?"

"I don't know." I threw up my arms, exasperated. "But . . ." I trailed off and started walking again.

"But what?" asked Peter, following after me.

I stopped and turned to him. "You're going to think I'm crazy," I said.

"I'm not going to think you're crazy. Just tell me."

"I feel like I can help them. Like I'm supposed to or something."

Peter slumped. "You don't need to worry about them," he said. "They'll manage without you."

"What if they can't?"

"Then it's not your problem."

"But if I can help?"

"Look, Ellie," he said with growing frustration I could see in his eyes. "They've survived how many years without you? They'll figure it out."

"What if they don't? And you heard what Levvi said. I'm running out of time."

Peter sighed. "Can't you just forget about it?"

"Fine," I said, turning to walk home.

Peter stood still as I walked ahead on the trail, and I was glad for it. I had been in a rotten mood all day and I knew arguing about this was going to make me cry. I didn't want him to see me like this.

"Wait up," he called after me. His footsteps were catching up, but I kept walking. "Wait, Ellie. Wait." He pulled on my arm to stop me. "I'm sorry. Don't be mad."

I stared at the ground, hiding my teary eyes from him.

"Are you crying?" he asked, pulling my chin up.

"No." I wiped at my eyes, feeling stupid.

"Oh, geez," said Peter. He pulled on his sleeve and wiped it across my cheek. "I'm sorry. I didn't mean to—"

"It's not you, Peter," I said, cutting him off. "I don't know what it is." I turned away from him again and kicked at the ground. "I just feel so strange lately. So freakin' lost or something."

Peter circled around to face me. "Hey," he said. "You're going to be okay. You just need to give it some time, ya know?"

"But I don't have time."

He sighed and reached for my hands, pulling them into his. "We should never have gone," he said.

I pulled away. "What do you want me to say? That you were right? I'm sorry, but how was I supposed to let all that go?"

"No. That's not what I meant. I don't know." He grabbed at his hair in frustration. "I just wish none of this ever happened."

"Well, it did," I said, feeling new tears stinging my eyes. "And now I've got to deal with it."

Peter sighed wearily, staring at me with his lips pressed tight. He tried for my hands again, but I pulled back and folded my arms over my chest.

"Look, maybe you should just go," I said. I didn't really want him to go, but I was exhausted and tired, and I didn't feel like talking about this anymore.

"Yeah, okay," he said, but he stood still and stared at me with his hands in his pockets.

"What?" I asked, feeling thin and papery and like my crabby, grumpy self was going to crack and bleed if scraped at too much longer.

"Ellie," he said, shrugging. "Just remember . . . they're not the only ones that need you."

I took a deep breath and pondered that thought quietly.

He shrugged at me again. "Okay . . . I guess I'll talk to you later."

Peter turned away. I stood alone in the forest and watched him walk until he faded among the trees and was out of sight.

I walked back home in a foul mood. It was still early, and a Saturday, and I only had myself to thank for the lonely evening I had to look forward to.

Dad and Millie were in the kitchen when I entered.

"What's this?" I asked, eyeing the counter with curiosity. There were about fifty empty beer bottles lined up on top of it.

"Your dad's getting into the beer business," said Millie. She was fiddling with the spout of a large white bucket sitting next to the bottles.

"Yep, brewing up some ale," said Dad.

"Now that's something I can see you doing," I said with a smile at Dad. "What are you going to call it? You'll need a good name if you want to stand out."

"It's just a hobby," said Dad.

I shrugged him off. "How about Old Papa Jim's Brewsky? Or . . . Jimmy's Over the Hill Brewing Company? Or Ol' Papa Hearts Best Brew."

"Ha . . . ha," Dad said without a smidge of a smile on his face.

Millie leaned into Dad and patted his back warmly. "Hey, fifty's not that old," she said. "You'll see when it starts creeping up on you." She winked at me.

"I'll keep thinking," I said, laughing at them. "Can I taste some?"

Dad eyed me sedately, mulling the thought. "One sip," he said and pushed a bottle to me.

I brought it to my lips. "Eww . . ." I stuck out my tongue and shuddered the vile taste away. "No offense, but is that how it's supposed to taste?"

"Yep," said Dad flatly. "And that's how it all tastes." He lowered stern eyebrows at me, warning me to stay away.

I put up my hands, happy to yield on this one.

"Where's Peter?" asked Millie.

I glanced at Peter's apple crisp, which still sat on the counter, cold and left. "Ah . . . he had to go home," I said, hoping I had managed to keep out any telltale signs there could be more to that story.

"Your dad and I are going to be watching a movie in a bit if you want to join us."

I pinched up my cheek, unsure. "Thanks . . . maybe," I said. "I think I'm just going to try and get some homework done, though."

"Okay," said Millie, perhaps sensing something was wrong, but thankfully she didn't ask.

I got up and reached across the counter and pulled the apple crisp to me. I grabbed the aluminum foil that was already out and pulled a piece over the top.

"This is Peter's," I said, putting it in the fridge.

"You're going to make apple crisp and not share it with your ol' father?" grumbled Dad.

I closed the fridge and walked back over to him. "There's an apple pie just for you, Dad," I said, kissing him on the cheek. "Four hundred degrees for forty-five minutes."

He patted my back. "Thank you, sweetheart."

I left Dad and Millie with their task of bottling the beer and headed to my room. I wasn't feeling like a movie night. I wasn't feeling like doing much of anything, really.

I flopped on my bed and gazed up through the skylight at the cloudless blue sky. There was a lone hawk hovering high in the air. He looked so free and so sure of his spot in the sky up there, and I watched, envious, wishing I could join him in his certitude.

I was feeling anything but sure these days. Restless, pulled, drained: that was how I was feeling. And the worst part was I couldn't do anything about it because I wasn't sure what I should do.

My unhelpful heart kept playing tricks on me. It was tugging, relentlessly, in both directions. It wanted Glacia. And it wanted home. At some point, it had split into two. I had split into two.

I felt now that maybe it was a long time coming. Maybe, somehow, Levvi was right and I did belong in Glacia. It was a strange idea that—with each passing day—was seeming not so strange after all.

And now that the split was complete, I was having to wrestle with these two sides of me. It was unsettling and frustrating, and I wanted—*needed*—it to stop.

I sat back up in my bed and looked across my room with wistful thoughts of Glacia. I slumped down and buried my head in my hands, wishing they'd go away.

22

"Is Peter coming to my party tonight?" asked Jenny.

We were at lunch, and I had been lost in a daze again. I rubbed at the corner of my tired eyes and glanced up at Jenny, who was tapping her pen at me. She had her notebook out and was busy making a playlist for the party.

"Oh, I'm not sure. I'll have to ask him after school. Is that okay?"

I had failed to mention that Peter and I hadn't spoken to each other in four days. He called me when he got home that night, but we both sat quietly, unsure of what to say, and it was just an uncomfortable, awkward mess the whole time. When he called the next day, I didn't pick up, and he hadn't tried again since. I was now feeling altogether like a lost dog, lonely and sad and very far from anything that resembled home. It sucked.

"Yeah, that's fine," she said, jotting down another song.

"What's wrong?" said Bethany. "Is he too scared to come hang out with us normals?"

She was sitting in the chair beside me, licking a spoon of yogurt. I turned a slow head and glared at her. I wasn't having it today. I was already on edge. I was already in a bad mood. And I had a pounding headache that would not stop, and now, thanks to Bethany, it just got a whole lot louder.

I steamed like a bull in her direction. "What's your problem, Bethany?" I snapped.

My sharp reaction caught her off guard. She turned slowly from her spoon to me. She lowered it to the table and kept hardline eyes on mine. "Sorry, I don't get it, Ellie," she said, raising her hands, looking incredulous. "I just don't understand why you like him."

"Why *wouldn't* I like him?" I shot back. "Do you even know him at all?" I wasn't bothering to control my volume, and a few kids from the tables beside us looked up. Good. They could stare for all I cared.

"Yeah, I *know* Peter Evans," she said, matching my volume. Her eyes rolled heavily in their sockets. "Everyone here *knows* Peter Evans." She made a gesture toward the crowded cafeteria. "He used to go here. Didn't he tell you?"

No. Peter never told me that.

"Yeah," she said, noticing my look of surprise. "And there's a reason he had no friends here. He's a loser like his two-timing, belligerent drunk of a father. I'd stay away from that family if I were you."

My eyes burned, hot with tears. I looked down, hating myself for it. I took a deep breath and sucked them up; I would not let her make me cry.

"He's not his father, Bethany. God!" I said, my frustration with her peaking. "You have no idea what you're talking about. And you don't know him. If you did, you would know he's actually pretty cool." I shook my head, realizing how exhausted I was. I liked

Bethany, I did, but I wasn't going to keep defending Peter to her. "Anyway, whatever. Think what you want, but he's my best friend, so I'm sorry, but if you can't accept him, I don't think we can be friends anymore." I turned away from Bethany and stared at my lunch tray, still trying to control my tears.

"I think he's cute," said a quiet Jenny from across the table. I glanced up to see her smiling face and was hit with a rush of gratitude. "Come on, Bethany. You've got to at least admit he's cute."

Bethany glowered at Jenny, then rolled defeated eyes over to me. "Fine," she said. "Yeah, he's not bad looking." Then she grumbled, low and under her breath, "He could use a haircut, though." She met my gaze. "Look, I'm sorry. You're right. I don't know him. I'll be nice."

"You're going to talk to him at the party tonight," I told her.

"What am I going to talk to him about?" she rasped.

"Just say hi to him. That's all," I said, finding my irritation with her once again.

"Fine," she said, and then more kindly added, "I can do that."

While I was waiting to board the bus after school, Jenny's crush, Joey Williams, walked past me.

"Hey, Joey!" I called after him.

He stopped and turned to me, confused. We had never spoken before, and I only knew him from science class. He pointed at himself awkwardly, checking to see if I had really meant him.

I nodded impatiently.

"Hey!" I said again, hoping he would hurry. My bus was filling up and the bus driver was starting to tap his foot at me.

"Ellie?" asked Joey, walking toward me.

"Yeah. So, hey, I don't know if you know this, but Jenny B's having her birthday party tonight—you should come."

"Are you asking me out?" he asked, obviously still confused as to why I was speaking to him.

"Oh, no. I'm sorry. I mean . . . just . . . you know, it would be cool if you came to *Jenny's* party." I tried to emphasize Jenny's name without being too obvious. "You know who she is, right?"

"Yeah, I know who Jenny is," he said. Of course he did. *Everybody here knows everybody.*

"Yeah, so you should come. It'd be fun. Starts at 7:30. Do you know where she lives?"

"Yeah, she lives on my street," he said.

"Oh, well, then that's perfect."

The bus driver waved for me to hurry.

"I got to go. I'll see you later at the party," I said, quickly climbing the steps.

"Wait, Ellie!" Joey called after me. The door closed on him as he was still trying to say something. I waved and smiled as the bus rolled away.

23

The key. I know it's in here somewhere.

I was searching through the top drawer of Dad's desk. The bus had just dropped me off, and I didn't have much time. I didn't know where Millie was, but her new car wasn't in the driveway. This was the first opportunity I had to try and get my locket since coming back from Glacia, and I needed to take the chance. It was now or never, I told myself.

I closed the drawer. That was too obvious. Where would Dad put it? I thought for a second, then continued my search in the small coat closet. This was where the safe had been hidden, but I hadn't seen a key anywhere. He had a few business jackets hanging in here. I checked the pockets. Nothing. I looked around the closet. It was fairly empty except for a single shoebox shelved at the top. I opened it. It was filled with letters addressed to Dad, from Millie—from the month they spent apart when she visited her family in Tennessee. Nope, I wouldn't be reading those. I put the box back.

He had some dress shoes lined up against the back of the closet. I picked one up and tipped it over. Nothing. I repeated this for the other shoes, and on the last loafer, a jangle of metal fell to the heel. I grabbed at the small brass keyring and hurried over to the lockbox.

I inserted the key, twisted, then opened the lid. The sealed envelope containing the locket was at the bottom. I grabbed it and placed it in my pocket.

Thinking quickly, I glanced around the room for the box of envelopes. I spotted it on a shelf near the door. I took a new envelope and was careful to put the box back on the shelf the same way I had found it.

Another search around the room and I spotted a jar of loose change. I grabbed a small handful and placed it in the envelope. I licked and sealed the paper and placed it in the safe.

I closed and locked the safe and had just finished placing it back at the bottom of the closet when the back door slammed shut.

I quickly deposited the key back in the shoe and ran on tiptoes out of the room.

"Ellie, are you home?" Millie called from downstairs. Worried my nervous voice would give me away, I pretended not to hear her and quickly scaled the steps to my room, then plopped on my bed in a heap of nerves.

"Hey, Ellie!" Millie called from downstairs. My nerves electrified at the sound of her voice.

I had been locked up in my room all afternoon. My guilt was keeping me prisoner. And now, I'd been caught. She knew. She went into the office and found something I had accidentally left behind. It was easy to work out why I had gone in there. In her hand was the envelope, jangling with the sound of coins, obviously containing a locket no more. I took a deep breath.

"Peter's here!" she called again. *Peter*—a whole new set of nerves circuited through me.

I released myself from my prison and ran down the stairs as fast as I could. I came into the kitchen. It was just Millie . . . at the stove.

"Where is he?"

"Waiting outside, hon," she said, not looking up from her sizzling pan.

I peeked out the kitchen window; Peter's legs, with his sneakered feet, were resting at the bottom of the porch steps.

"Thanks, Millie."

"What are you doing here?" I asked as I opened the door.

Peter got to his feet and stepped up on the porch to stand beside me. "Um, I don't know. Just thought I'd come say hi," he said, sounding unsure. He lowered his gaze to his feet. I stared happily at his messy hair.

"Hi," I murmured softly.

He raised his head. "Hey," he said back.

We quietly stared at each other through the murky wall of tension that hung heavy between us.

"So you finally got it?" Peter asked after a moment.

"What?"

"The locket," he said, pointing at my neck.

"Oh, crap!" I screeched. I hurriedly tucked it under my shirt. "Oh my god! Millie could have seen that!" I shook my head in disbelief at my stupidity.

"So you're going," he said, his voice flat with no judgment.

"I don't know," I said honestly. "Maybe . . . maybe not. Can we talk about it?"

He nodded. "Yeah, that's why I came."

A tight band snapped and released from around my chest. I took a happy breath. "I'm glad you did," I said. "I was starting to miss your cute freckles."

Peter reached up to touch his nose. A hint of a smirk peeked out from behind his hand. "Starting to?" he baited.

I shook my head with what I knew was too goofy of a smile, being too big and obvious on my face. "Do you want to sit?" I asked, tilting my head toward the porch swing.

We sat together, the rusty chains creaking under our weight. We slowly pushed with our feet and the swing rocked in motion. It was a warm day that carried the smell of fresh spring mud in the breeze, and I wished life could be as easy as sitting here with Peter on a day just like this.

Peter turned to me. "I want to help you, Ellie," he said.

"Yeah, I know you do," I said with wretched regret for having made him feel bad about it. "I'm really sorry I've been so weird about all of this. I'm just having a tough time shaking it."

Peter pointed to the chain around my neck. "It doesn't look like you're trying to shake it," he said, but his tone wasn't angry; it was just the same flat note, working to further push the guilt down, tamping it tight in my stomach until it hurt.

I tucked my hands under my legs and kicked them out in front of me. I pulled my shoulders into a shrug. "Yeah, well, what can I say? I'm a split girl these days. But part of me is trying." I sighed wearily. "I promise." I looked down, shaking my head at my two selves and a little at Peter for not getting it. But what did I expect? *Who* could get this?

Peter turned on the swing to face me. "So let's figure it out," he said. "If you can't let it go, if you really feel like you need to help them, then maybe we can find a solution that doesn't involve you giving up your *whole* life, ya know?" Peter scoffed a little and turned back to sit straight.

I stared at him, chewing my lip. *Giving up my whole life.* Of course, that was what he had been worried about. "Peter, I wasn't going to stay there—not forever."

"Yeah, but that's what they want," he said, shaking his head.

"I know, but . . ." I paused and lingered in a battle with myself. This innate need to help them came with the gut feeling that I could do it without sacrificing everything. But I had no idea how I was going to accomplish that, and another feeling, bouncy and bothersome, told me I would still help no matter what. I sighed, still caught in my struggle.

"I don't know why you trust them so much," said Peter, "or why you care so much about them."

"I don't know, either," I said. How was I ever going to explain to him the feeling of responsibility that had come over me for this strange world? I couldn't even explain it to myself. I sat back on the swing, feeling the murky wall rise between us again.

"Look," said Peter after a moment, "I didn't come here to fight.

I promise." He looked at me with pleading eyes. "But, Ellie, they're wrong. I just know it."

"Okay," I said, heeding the strained plea in his voice. "How are they wrong?"

"For one thing, they're wrong about your grandmother," he said. "Granny Leira was really sweet. She wasn't like what they said. I can't see her betraying anyone like that. She was probably the least selfish person—besides you—that I've ever known. And," he said, his voice rising with disdain, "I really doubt her only motive for bringing you here . . . was so you could help *them*." He shook his head and fell between his knees with a sigh, pressing at his temples in frustration.

I stared at him slumped and slouched in the swing. "You don't like them very much, do you?"

"Not really, Ellie. Can you blame me?" he asked. He pulled his hands from his face and looked at me, bruised and hurt.

My breath caught, and I floundered in my stupidity. I wanted to turn my hand around and slap some sense into myself. These strange Glacians, whom I was so eager to help, had been nothing but mean bullies to him—to Peter, whom I knew I would help, without hesitation, if *he* were in trouble. But did he know that?

"Oh God, Peter. I'm so sorry," I said. "I really am. They were awful to you. You know I don't think that was okay, right? I just—"

"Yeah, I know," he said, stopping me, but he still sounded hurt. "Anyway, Ellie, there's more."

"Okay. Like what?"

"Well, I just don't think they need you like they say. If Razora can become queen, then shouldn't it be possible for someone else? They're missing a piece here. I just know it."

"So what are you thinking?"

"Ellie, did Granny Leira leave you anything? Maybe some kind of clue as to what she wanted from you."

I thought about that, but I couldn't think of anything except the locket. "I don't know," I said. "The house was full of stuff. How would I know what to even look for?" And then I remembered something. "The note!"

"A note?"

"Yeah, I mean, it's probably nothing, but she left me a note. It was from her, handwritten and everything."

"What did it say?"

"Not much really, just . . . um . . ." I tried to think of the words.

"Well, do you still have it?"

"Yeah, I do, actually. I'll go get it."

I got up and ran into the house. I sprinted to my room and took the note from where I had placed it safely in my journal. I hurried back down the stairs and handed it to Peter. He read it with a smile on his face.

"I miss her," he said and folded the paper back up. "Can I hang on to this? I feel like there's something here."

"Yeah, keep it as long as you need, but . . . I don't have much—"

"You don't have much time," he finished for me. "I know."

We sat quietly for a few minutes, listening to the creaky swing playing its oddly soothing creaky song. I twisted in my seat and stared at Peter, chewing on my lip and counting his new spring freckles.

"What's up?" he asked.

"So, hey," I said. I was a little nervous; he wasn't going to like this question.

"Yeah?" prodded Peter.

"So . . . I'm going to Jenny's party tonight. I was wondering if you wanted to come." I already knew what his answer would be, but I still wanted to try.

"Oh, I don't know, Ellie," he said, shifting uncomfortably. "I don't think that's such a good idea."

"Why not?"

He looked at me with eyes way up in their sockets.

"Come on . . . It won't be that bad." I smiled sympathetically. "I'll be there, and . . ." I shrugged because that was the best case I had for getting him to come with me. I bumped his shoulder, hoping to bump a yes out of him.

"Ugh . . ." groaned Peter. "Okay, I guess."

"Yeah?"

"Yes, Cordelia, I'll go with you." He grinned slyly.

"Oh God," I said, shaking my head. "Are you going to start calling me that?"

"It's nice," he teased.

I scowled at him, unamused. I held my tongue, not wanting to give him the pleasure of a response. He was still smiling.

I shook my head at him. "So you'll really go?" I asked.

He nodded reluctantly. "If you really want me to," he said.

I smiled happily. "I really do."

24

"Ellie!" Millie called from downstairs. "Peter's here!"

I was finishing getting dressed for the party. I had decided to wear a pair of navy leggings with a bulky yellow sweater that had a ridiculously high turtleneck. It was a gift from Millie from last Christmas. Not my favorite style, but she would be happy to see me in it and it would be just the thing for hiding my locket.

"Hey, Peter," I said, entering the kitchen. He was talking to Millie by the door.

"Hey," he said, turning to me. He was wearing a blue T-shirt and his usual pair of jeans, though they were pressed and free from the usual wrinkles now, and his hair was combed and out of his face, exposing his cute eyes and freckles. He walked over to me and a spicy scent of sandalwood and musk, not usually there, drifted to my nose.

"Do I look okay?" he whispered into my ear nervously.

I smiled at him. "Yeah," I said, leaning in and whispering back. "You don't need to worry about that—they all think you're cute." He shot his head back doubtfully. I laughed at him and nodded, confirming he'd heard me right.

"Hey, you're wearing the sweater I bought you!" exclaimed Millie. She moved to stand beside me and reached out to touch the fabric along my arm. "It looks great on you. Doesn't she look great, Peter?"

"Yeah, she looks great," said Peter, smiling at me.

"Thanks," I said, bowing my head to hide my blushed cheeks.

"Your dad's going to drive you two over," said Millie.

I listened for Dad's footsteps upstairs, thinking I heard a scuffle in his office. My body tensed as I tried to get a fix on his location. He was heading down the stairs now—*phew*. Being a criminal sure was stressful. I would be putting the locket back as soon as possible.

"You two just about ready?" called Dad as he entered the kitchen.

"I think we're ready. Peter?" I asked.

"Yep," he said. Then, under his breath, he added, "As ready as I'll ever be."

Jenny's house was situated in one of the nicer neighborhoods in Ocean Lake. It was one of those neighborhoods where everybody kept tidy lawns and had big garages housing polished cars.

"Hey, Ellie!" Jenny shouted with a swing of the door. "You're late!"

"I'm so sorry! Did I get the time wrong? I thought it started at 7:30. No?"

"Oh, that's . . ." She trailed off with her mouth gaping wide. "Oh my god," she whispered. "What is Joey Williams doing here?" She was looking past me to the outside.

Joey was walking up the stoop with one of his buddies from school.

I smiled big. "Um, oh yeah. I kind of forgot to tell you, but I invited Joey."

"What!" she exclaimed. She fixed on me. "You invited Joey Williams? How?"

"I just asked him," I said. "And you should probably stop calling him Joey Williams. Just Joey is good."

Jenny smiled gleefully and gave me a big hug. "You have no idea how happy I am right now, Ellie. I could just kiss you." She then pushed me aside as Joey entered the house.

"Hey, Joey Williams," she said sweetly to him.

I laughed at her, then turned to Peter. "Come on," I said, motioning for him to follow me. "I think that's our cue to leave."

We passed through the dimly lit living room where a bunch of kids from school crowded around. Many curious eyes looked up at Peter as we walked by, and I took his hand to pull him along faster.

Bethany was sitting at the kitchen counter, talking with some girls from school when we entered.

"Hi, Bethany," I said.

"Oh, hey!"

"You remember Peter?"

"Oh yeah, of course," she said, looking at him with a friendly smile. "Hey, Peter. It's good to see you again." I was happy to hear no hint of sarcasm in her voice.

"Hi," said Peter, shyly tucking his hands into his pockets.

"Are you guys hungry? There's plenty of pizza," said Bethany, gesturing to the stack of pizza boxes sitting on the counter beside her.

"I could eat." I grabbed paper plates and put a few slices of pepperoni on them for Peter and myself. Peter eagerly grabbed at the pizza and shoved it into his mouth.

"You hungry?" I asked, laughing at him.

"Not really," he said through a mouthful of cheese.

The kitchen door swung open, and a nervous and panicking Jenny came rushing in.

"Oh my gosh, you guys," she said, her voice shaky with nerves.

"What's going on?" asked Bethany.

"Joey's here!" she screeched, informing Bethany of the news.

"What! Really?"

"Yeah," she said. "What do I do? I didn't know what to talk about, so I just walked away. He's a lot quieter than he is at school." She looked at us desperately. Then she turned to Peter. "You're a boy. What do I do?"

Peter stared back, unsure. "Um, I don't know," he said with a shrug. "Maybe play a game, or how about dancing? You know, so you don't have to talk."

"Oh my gosh!" said Jenny. "Yeah, a dance floor! That's a great idea! Thanks!" She bounced over to Peter and hugged him. "Do I ask him?" She consulted Peter again.

He was smiling awkwardly and looked utterly amused that she was asking him for advice. "Wait," he said. "At first . . . just in case he wants to ask you."

"Okay, good idea. But you guys got to start dancing first, or else no one else will."

"I'll get the music," said Bethany. She ran to the living room and cranked up the volume on the stereo, then was back at the door. "Peter!" she called. "Help me with this coffee table."

They cleared a space in the living room for a dance floor. A peppy dance song played loudly across the room.

"Come on, guys!" said Jenny. She motioned for me and Peter to get up and start dancing.

Peter shook his head in disbelief. "I have no idea why I suggested this," he said. "I don't even know how to dance."

"Neither do I." I laughed. "Come on . . . it'll be fun." I grabbed Peter's hand and dragged him to the floor.

Thankfully, Bethany had taken it upon herself to go around the room and persuade others to join in. It wasn't long before the makeshift dance floor was covered with dozens of amateur dancers who looked just as awkward as we felt.

Joey walked up to Jenny, who was standing in the corner. He took her hand and walked her onto the dance floor.

"Hey, look," I said to Peter. "It worked." He smiled, seeing Jenny and Joey dancing together.

We danced awkwardly and happily to the song. Then the music switched over to a slow ballad and the dance floor began to clear.

"Um . . ." I said, unsure if we should follow. I started to turn. Peter grabbed my hand to stop me.

"Can I have this dance?" he asked.

"Sure," I said with a happy smile.

Peter put his arms around my waist. I followed his lead and reached my arms up around him, suddenly feeling nervous.

We swayed slowly to the music. It felt really good to be here with Peter and not worrying about crazy stuff that was out of my control. I took a deep breath and exhaled, letting myself relax in the moment.

"Normal feels really good tonight," I said.

"This isn't normal for me," said Peter with a smile.

"I'm glad you came, though."

"Yeah, me too."

"Are you having *any* fun?"

"I always have fun with you, Ellie," he said.

I smiled at him, feeling the same. "I think you've made a friend in Jenny, at least." I gestured to where Jenny and Joey were dancing beside us.

"Yeah." He laughed, but he shook his head. "That was all you, though," he said. "You're a really good friend, Ellie. We're lucky you moved here."

"I don't know about that," I said, brushing him off.

"I do," he said. He stared at me, his eyes narrowed and anxious. "You're the best thing that's ever happened to me." He paused. "And I'm really scared I'm going to lose you."

"Peter, you're not. I promise. Okay?" But for some reason, my words seemed weak and unsure. I hoped he didn't notice.

"Okay," he said, eyeing me with suspicion. "That better be true." He studied my face again. "I know I sound selfish, Ellie, but it's not just me. What would your dad do if you left?"

"Yeah, I know," I said. I did know. Dad would be heartbroken, especially after losing Mom. I couldn't do that to him.

We continued stepping slowly with the music.

"Peter," I said.

"Yeah?"

"I'm lucky, too."

"How's that?" he asked.

I reached up and gently touched his forehead, rubbing my thumb over the memory. I smiled at him. "I'm lucky to have collided with you on that fateful day."

Peter laughed. "Yeah, that's exactly what we did, huh?"

"Yeah," I said, laughing. "And I knew you were special. I knew that very first day." He narrowed his eyes doubtfully. I ignored it. "Do you know how I knew?"

"No, I don't know," he said with a quiet chuckle.

I smiled, thinking back. "I was sitting at the gazebo. You came out of the diner . . . and you held the door for an elderly couple . . . and you had a big smile on your face . . . just completely happy to be helping. It was really sweet."

"I don't remember that," he said.

"Oh, and the Advil . . ." I added. "That was really nice." I smiled, remembering. "Oh, and the Twix."

"The Twix?" asked Peter.

"Yeah, you took my suggestion on the Twix. I thought that was cool."

"Oh yeah," he said. "Can I tell you a secret?"

I nodded.

He leaned into my ear and whispered, "I just really like Twix."

25

The bell chimed when I entered Carle's. It had been sprinkling a little when I left the house, but a downpour ensued just as I reached town, and I was soaked through and through as I entered the store.

"Hey," said Peter with a chuckle when he saw me. We had planned to meet here, and he was waiting for me by the door.

Water ran down in beads off the ends of my clothes and hair, creating a drippy mess on the floor beneath me. "You're soaking wet," he said, stating the obvious.

He was completely dry and was holding an umbrella.

"You couldn't have brought that to me?"

"Sorry, I didn't see you out there." He laughed again.

I glowered at him, still laughing. "Are you done?"

Peter smiled and took my hand. "Let's do this, Cordelia," he said, pulling me by the hand to the candy aisle.

The plan was to get a bunch of snacks and spend the rainy Sunday playing video games. I was looking forward to vegging out and doing nothing. I was hoping I could get my mind to calm down.

My anxiety was growing with each passing day, and although I was trying, I couldn't seem to get Glacia out of my head.

"So, Ellie," said Peter as he put some chips into our basket.

"Yeah?"

"My mom wants to meet you."

I looked at him, happy. "Finally. And you're actually going to let me?"

"Eh . . . I guess. She said if I'm going to be hanging out with you so much, she should at least know what you look like."

I jumped up and clapped my hands. "I'd love to meet her," I said. "Why don't we go now?"

"Now?"

I was nodding happily.

"I guess," he said with a shrug.

"Oh, yay!" I cheered. Then a nervous wave hit. "Do you think she's going to like me, though?"

He smiled. "Yeah," he said. "I think she's going to like you."

We paid for our stuff and headed over. It was still raining, and Peter and I had to duck under the umbrella together. It didn't serve much purpose for me since I was already soaked, but he insisted on sharing anyway.

The walk to Peter's house was easy. He lived on the other side of town, just outside the main strip, and we were able to cut through a couple of puddle-ridden parking lots to reach his street.

He lived in a busy neighborhood with lots of houses clustered together. His house was small, with weathered wood instead of paint. It sat a few feet from the street in a small yard with a trove of bushes padding the perimeter.

The rainy day had made a horrific mix with the last of the snow, and we walked up a muddy, slushy driveway. I followed Peter as he led the way up the wooden porch situated on the side of the house.

"Mom!" he called. We entered a small kitchen. It was tiny, the whole thing smaller than Millie's big closet, but it was clean with little clutter on the countertops and an empty sink wiped dry.

A black Labrador came running through an open door, followed by a small boy clad in a diaper. The boy babbled nonsense as he ran and waved a toy car in the air. He and the dog charged at Peter's legs in unison.

"Peta, Peta!" he shouted.

"Hey, buddy." Peter picked up the wiggly child and held him in his arms. "Ellie, this is Liam and that's Shadow." He gestured to the dog that was jumping around at his feet. Liam looked like a tiny version of Peter. He stretched out his arm and handed me his toy.

"Hi, Liam! Aren't you a cutie!" I said, smiling at the boy. Liam smiled back happily, then began to squirm, and Peter put him back down to cruise around the kitchen with the dog.

A dryer door slammed shut, and a moment later, a pretty, petite woman who looked a few years younger than Millie walked in. She had mousy brown hair tied back in a messy bun and wore tattered clothes smelling of bleach.

"Hey, Mom. This is Ellie," said Peter.

"Ellie!" his mom exclaimed. A delighted smile spread across her face. "Oh, it's really good to finally meet you." She stretched out her hand to me. "You'll have to excuse my appearance. I was trying to get a few chores done before work. Had I known you were *coming*"—she eyed Peter with a sideways sneer—"I would have cleaned up a bit."

"That's okay." I shook her hand. "It's nice to meet you, too," I said. It wasn't until that moment that I realized how much I wanted her to like me, and my words oozed out sweet like honey in hopes that I could charm her.

She eyed us both with a smile. "So, what are you two up to today?"

"We just wanted to come say hi," answered Peter.

"Would you like to stay for dinner, Ellie?"

"No, Mom, we had plans today. I don't think we were going to stay long."

"Oh, that's okay, Peter. We can play here. I just need to let my dad know."

"Do you need to borrow the phone?" asked Mrs. Evans.

"That's okay. I can text him." I dug my phone out of my back pocket.

"Oh, you have a cell phone," said Mrs. Evans. "Peter has been bugging me for one of those ever since you moved in." She playfully pinched Peter's cheek.

"Mom!" said Peter swiftly, lowering his head to hide his embarrassment. I laughed at him. "Mom, you can't do dinner. Don't you work tonight?" he asked, attempting to change the subject.

"Yeah, I have to go in, but I can stay for a few bites if we eat early." She paused, and an anxious breath fluttered through her lips. "I should probably get started on that now, though." Her cheery face swiftly turned glum, and she shrank, slumped and frazzled, suddenly looking completely overwhelmed. She turned to Peter. "Can you take Liam with you guys so I can work on dinner?"

"Sure." Peter shrugged and grabbed Liam as he passed under our feet.

We turned the corner in the kitchen, and Peter paused at the bottom of the stairs. "Your dad would be okay if we hang out in my room, as long as Liam's with us, right?" he asked, looking unsure. "Or maybe not?" His expression was so serious it had me inwardly laughing a little. He was still stopped and waiting for my answer.

"I think that'd be okay," I said, smiling at him and making a mental note to mention this thoughtfulness to Dad at some point.

We entered the room and Peter closed the door behind him, preventing Liam from scampering off. His room was clean and tidy with a made bed and vacuumed carpet. There were multiple *Star Wars* posters on his walls with matching figurines orderly arranged on top of a pine dresser. There was a basket of neatly folded laundry in one corner of the room, and a small, wooden bookshelf sat against the wall near the door. Liam moved to the piles of CDs and books stacked inside and was taking it upon himself to remove them one by one from the shelf.

"It's not usually this clean in here," said Peter. "My mom did this."

"At least you're honest," I said with a laugh. "It's a good thing I don't have to worry about you seeing *my* messy room."

Peter laughed.

I scanned the room and turned my attention to a stack of booklets on his dresser. "Hey, are these your comics?"

"Oh, yeah."

"Can I look?"

"Sure," said Peter, sounding a little hesitant.

I flipped through the pages. The one I was reading had a dopey kid that looked like a cross between Peter Parker and Harry Potter with similar round spectacles. He wore a backpack and was using a cell phone that shot lasers to fight an alien for his spaceship.

The kid stood small next to the big alien creature, but with a thrust of his laser phone, he shouted, "One small step for me, one giant kick in the butt for you!" He did a karate chop move with the laser in hand, and the alien fell flat and dead.

On the next page, the kid was piloting the craft and battling a dark cloud monster near the sun. The monster threatened to block the light from the world below, and the kid, now donning a pair of radiation-repelling sunglasses, defeated the monster with his laser light phone, saving the world.

"Oh my god, Peter, these are really good," I said, admiring the bright colors and well-done lines of his artwork. He was much better than he led me to believe.

"Thanks," he said. "How 'bout you?" He was standing beside me with a bundle of clothes in his hand.

"How 'bout me what?" I asked, still flipping through the pages.

"Do you have any new drawings you've been working on?"

"Oh, yeah, but . . ." I trailed off.

"But what?"

I smiled at him with flushed cheeks. "Um . . . I'm probably not going to be sharing my journal with you anymore," I said. No, I was not. Not with how many times his name now appeared among the doodles.

He laughed. "And why is that?"

I glanced over to see him smirking. I stared back down at the comic, shaking my head. "Nuh-uh," I said.

"What?" he asked, pretending like he didn't already know.

"Nope," I said. I wasn't going to give him the satisfaction of hearing me say it.

Peter laughed. "Well, you're going to have to make a book with just your sketches so I can see them."

I nodded at him. "Good idea," I said with a laugh, still looking down and still feeling my hot scarlet cheeks.

"Here," said Peter. He was handing over the wad of clothes in his hands.

"What?"

"You gotta get out of those wet clothes," he said, pushing the dry ones into my arms.

"Oh, thanks."

I found the bathroom just a room over and changed.

We sat back on the bed and watched as Liam continued his work of reorganizing the bookshelf. I looked at the floor and noticed, among the mess, that he had pulled out a yearbook from school.

"Hey," I said. "How come you never told me you used to go to my school?"

"Ah," said Peter, looking a little guilty and embarrassed as he noticed the yearbook. "I don't know. Not too many fond memories from that place. I don't know why I keep that thing."

"I'm sorry, Peter," I said, turning cross-legged on the bed to face him. He was slumped and fiddling with the corner of his pillowcase. I gently nudged him with my stockinged foot.

He looked up with somber eyes. "Don't say sorry to me, Ellie," he said. "I mean, you're the last person that should be saying sorry to me."

I shrugged and stared back at him. "I'm sorry because it's shitty and unfair. And I know how they are there . . . and I don't do anything about it."

"You're here with me now, Ellie." He squeezed my foot beside him. "Still real," he said with a sweet smile.

"I'm only here because you're adorable," I said. "There was no other motive."

Peter smiled, his eyes lifting happily. "I'll take that."

I sat back beside Peter, bumping his shoulder. I breathed a shaky breath, desperately wishing this moment—easy and happy with Peter—could just be enough. But my unsettled heart was still split.

An anxious tension pulsed through my body. I stretched out my legs in frustration and wrapped my fingers tightly around the back of my neck, trying to stifle a scream.

"What's the matter?" asked Peter.

"Oh, nothing. I think it's just this rainy weather getting to me, that's all."

He sighed. "No, it's Glacia, huh?"

I shifted uncomfortably. "Yeah. I don't know why. I can't explain it to you."

"You don't have to explain it to me," he said. "I get it."

I smiled at him, but it faltered. I took a shaky breath, releasing it in a slow stream to try and calm my nerves.

"Come on. Don't let it get to you so much." He sat up and faced me on the bed. "I'm going to figure it out for you. I just need another day or two. The answer is in Granny Leira's letter. I just know it."

"Peter, I don't think so." I didn't understand what he expected to find in that short letter. "We need to come up with another idea. Maybe Levvi's found something new. Or maybe we can read the law like you said. There might be something there."

"Yeah, maybe." He looked at me with tired eyes. "What do you suppose we do?"

"I want to go back."

"So you *do* plan on going back?" He took a bitter breath.

"Yeah. I think I have to," I said. "How else am I going to help?"

"Come on, Ellie. I really don't think it's such a good idea."

"I know you don't. I don't know why, but I just feel like I have to. It's my responsibility to help them." The words came out before I knew what I was even saying.

"Agh!" cried Peter. He buried his head in his hands, pulling at his hair in frustration. "It's *not* your responsibility!"

"I feel like it is," I said. I couldn't explain it more than that. Not even to myself. It was a sick gut feeling deep inside that pestered me and made me want to retch, and I knew helping Glacia was the only thing that would get it to go away.

Peter sighed wearily. "When did you want to go?"

"So you'll come?"

"Yeah. I'm not going to let you go there all by yourself."

"Why don't we go tonight?" I suggested.

"Tonight? I don't know, Ellie. Don't you think we should wait until we've thought it through a little more?"

"Like how?" I asked, now getting annoyed.

"I don't really know. We need some sort of plan, though. Don't you think?"

"I figured we could just make it up as we go."

"That's not a very smart plan."

"I didn't say it was. But I need to do something. I'm tired of just sitting around. It's driving me crazy." I let out a heavy sigh and moved off the bed to pace the room.

"I can't go tonight. It's a school night. My mom isn't going to let me stay at your house."

"Then when?" I snapped impatiently. "Friday?"

"This weekend's no good. I start visitations with my dad. What about next weekend?"

"I can't wait that long." How long would another week be for Glacia? "Maybe I could just go without you."

"Don't be stupid. That's crazy."

"I'll be fine."

"Ellie, look at me." Peter got up to stand beside me. He put his hands on my shoulders, forcing me to stop pacing. I stopped and stared into his worried eyes. "You can't go alone," he pleaded. "We know nothing about those people. I really don't think it's safe there."

"I'll be all right, Peter. They aren't going to hurt me."

"You don't know that. You know nothing about them."

"I can trust Levvi."

"How can you know that?"

"I don't know," I said with a shrug. "I just know." My trust in Levvi was another pesky gut feeling. Easy to listen to, but hard to explain.

Peter sighed and removed his hands from my shoulders. He slumped onto the bed. "Why do you have to be so stubborn?" he said, shaking his head.

I sat quietly beside him.

"I didn't think you would do something so stupid. You owe them nothing and you have a lot of people here that love you . . . your dad and Millie . . ." He paused. "And me." He kicked at a book on the carpet. "How can you be so careless?"

His voice came out bruised and broken. Whether it was his intention or not, it had worked to stir the guilt. A bitter taste rose in my throat, and it was strong.

"I didn't ask you to love me," I said, tears filling my eyes.

"Yeah, you kind of did," he said. He looked at me, pleading. "Just wait till Friday. I'll get out of it with my dad, and we can go together."

"I'm going tonight, Peter." I didn't realize I had made up my mind until I'd said it.

"What?" His eyes turned hard with disbelief.

"I'm sorry, but I have to."

"So there's no talking you out of it? You're just going to disregard everything I just said?"

"No. I'm listening to you . . . I am . . . I just—"

"You just don't care." He finished the sentence, throwing a disdainful look toward me. He moved from the bed, grabbing Liam, and left the room with a loud slam of the door.

I sat for a few moments, quiet and alone. Tears brimmed and poured salty streams down my face. I wiped them away and got up.

I pulled on my jeans and threw the sweatpants Peter had given me on the bed, then bundled my soaked shirt in my arms and left the room, still wearing his hoodie.

I stopped on the bottom step. Peter and his mom were talking in the kitchen. I took a deep breath and walked in.

"I'm really sorry, Mrs. Evans, but my dad wants me home," I lied.

"Oh, well, that's okay," she said with an understanding smile. "We'll do it another time."

"See you later, Peter," I said, bowing my head as I crossed the kitchen.

"Wait. Hold up," he shouted after me.

I didn't stop. Tears were building in my eyes again, and I didn't want him to see how pathetic I looked.

I ran outside as fast as I could, but he caught up to me in the driveway.

"Ellie, wait! I'm sorry. I shouldn't have stormed out like that."

I stopped for him but didn't turn. A drizzle of rain fell around us, working to saturate my clothes all over again.

"You don't have to go," said Peter. He was right behind me.

With my back still to him, I stifled my cries. "It's probably better if I did. We can talk tomorrow. Meet me at Carle's after school."

"Yeah, okay," he said.

There was a soft tap on my arm. I looked down to see the umbrella. Peter hooked it over my wrist, pulling it slightly. "Take it," he muttered.

I grabbed the umbrella and started to cry again. "Bye, Peter," I said, and without looking back, I walked off.

26

"Ugh," I groaned. I fumbled for my cell phone in the dark. My eyes were puffy and stuck, and there was a dull pressure in my forehead from my stuffy sinuses. I smacked my hand across the floor, finding the smooth plastic of my phone. I squinted at the bright light as I turned it on—12:17, and no missed calls from Peter.

With a sigh, I fell back to the mattress. I was lying fully dressed on top of my blankets. After coming back from Peter's, I had gone straight to my room and cried a blubbery mess into my pillow. And now, as I woke, the memory of our fight was rushing back, and a thick sinister ocean began to rise and crash awful in my stomach. *Oh God.* I was going to puke.

I pulled the pillow out from under my head and covered my face, trying to stop the sludge of regret from rising and spewing from my mouth.

What was my problem? Why was I being so "stubborn"? I wasn't trying to be. "I'm not," I mumbled into my pillow, still arguing with Peter, who couldn't hear me right now.

The weight, the burden, the feeling of responsibility that had come over me—it was relentless. It pulled. It pressed on my heart, and I was reaching the breaking point. This was it. I couldn't go on feeling like this. It was too much.

I pulled the pillow down, staring into my quiet room with the only answer that felt even slightly right.

I would help. I had to. I wouldn't sacrifice my life. I wouldn't leave Dad or Peter, but I would help. I would try, at least. And if I was going to help, it would need to be soon. It would need to be now.

I opened my door at the bottom of the stairs and crept down the hall. The house was silent. Dad and Millie were asleep. I quietly made my way to the kitchen and slid on my boots.

The back door creaked as I opened it. "No, no, no," I whispered. I stopped for a second to listen for footsteps upstairs. It was quiet. I stepped outside and carefully closed the door behind me, praying desperately it would be silent. It was kind and creaked just a little.

Once outside, I dashed across the yard, toward the trails. With my adrenaline in high doses, I ran the distance between my house and the lake swiftly. It wasn't long before I was standing at the water's edge. Small waves splashed now, and there was little ice.

I couldn't delay. I stepped in.

The icy water hit my skin like tiny blades, piercing deep and numbing my bones. I had my eye on the boulder, just a few more feet out. The water stiffened me cold, removing my breath as it reached my stomach, then my chest. Then a few more steps and I was there. I took a moment to breathe, then lowered, dipping the point of the heart into the water.

In an instant, a circle of light sprung forth, and I descended.

Coming to a stop at the bottom, the elevator opened into a dark, cavernous foyer. It was quiet. The bright lights from the elevator had left me blind, and I was unprepared for the darkness as the door solidified closed. I waited anxiously for my eyes to adjust.

A dull lavender light emitted from the mass of pools scattered on the ground around me. It was just enough for shapes to form, and with my adjusted eyes, I now looked upon an empty cavern. There were no mermaids or unicorns in sight.

Something was wrong. Throughout the room, chunks of crystal had been knocked from the walls. There was an enormous boulder that had been cut from the ceiling above, and it now lay haphazardly in the middle of a stone path. A bridge in the center of the room was missing a rail, with the sunken remains in the water below.

I navigated through the lobby and toward the archway in the back, being careful not to trip on any debris. As I crossed under the waterfall, I thought I heard the swirling *whoosh* of the elevator.

I stopped and stared into the darkness. "Who's there?" I called. My voice rebounded, echoing a chorus in the empty room. The waterfall behind me crashed loudly on the stone floor, and I couldn't be sure if anyone answered. My nerves electrified and danced on the surface of my skin as I waited in the shadows, but no one appeared.

With shaky knees, I continued through the archway. There was no source of light in the long corridor, and the dim glow of the pools didn't reach far. Soon, all light faded, and the darkness was complete.

I ran my hands along the edge of the wall, letting it guide me. I felt an opening and turned down a connecting corridor. A faint line of light glowed dimly in the distance, drawing me forward. As

I moved closer, the walls came into focus and the silhouettes of my hands in front of me sharpened.

I stopped at an exceptionally large door, big and grand and made of dark, unpolished wood. It reminded me of the doors from the barn outside my house. It split down the middle the same way, with one side left ajar. A dull blue light escaped from within.

I peered inside.

"Whoa," I marveled quietly, stepping back in awe. I took a steadying breath and stepped inside.

The room, from wall to wall, was a vast expanse of green meadow that stretched for several acres all around. Though it felt like I had walked outside, I could clearly see stone walls rising high in the distance. There was a forest of big pine trees along the perimeter of the wall, creating a woodsy enclosure where hundreds of unicorns grazed and slept. The ground all around was lush grass and the sky above was sparkling with stars. *How is this possible?* I stared in wonderment at the spectacle in front of me.

There was a slosh, and I looked over to see a unicorn drinking from a babbling brook. I recognized his silver mane and horn. It was Midnight.

I walked over to the magical creature. He lifted his sparkling blue eyes to me.

"Hey, boy," I said, extending my hand to him.

Midnight nudged his big nose into my shoulder, and I put my arms around his strong neck. "I missed you, too," I said softly to him. His warmth immediately comforted me, and I felt safe by his side.

"Midnight," I whispered, "do you know how I can find Levvi? I really need to talk to him."

The unicorn lowered his horn with a bow, and the tip emitted a low light that briefly buzzed, then shut off. He then nuzzled his nose around my neck, and I waited, understanding that Levvi was on his way.

A few moments later, someone called my name. "Ellie?" I turned toward the door and saw Levvi walking to meet me.

"Levvi!" I shouted. I ran to him and wrapped my arms tightly around him.

"You came back," he said, surprised.

"Yeah, I did, huh?"

We held on for another moment, then let go.

I studied Levvi with a weary heart. He was older. His hair was longer, and his jaw and cheekbones were more defined. And though his smooth skin would still be considered young, his once youthful eyes had hardened and aged, and they held the heaviness of life's burdens behind them now. "How long has it been?" I asked.

"Last I saw you, my princess"—he paused to think—"was twenty-seven years ago."

I gulped. "I'm sorry it took me so long. I wasn't sure what to do." I lowered my head, ashamed.

"You need not be sorry, my princess." He smiled kindly. "I did not expect to see you here at all. Are you sure of your decision to come?"

"No," I said. "I'm *not* sure. I want to help, but I can't stay."

Levvi's eyes dropped, and a broken and distraught merman was in front of me. All the uncertainty and confusion I had been feeling over the past few weeks surged in my soul and I began to cry.

He raised his head and looked at me with compassion. "I am

sorry for this hefty burden we have placed upon you, my princess. Please know it is not your duty to save us."

"Is it not?" I asked, taken aback.

"No. Contrary to what some here might think, it is not." He paused, averting his eyes shamefully. "We merfolk here in Glacia only have ourselves to blame for our current state. We alone are the makers and keepers of our problems. It was unfair of us to ask what we did. I see that now, and I am truly sorry." He slumped into an apologetic bow.

"But I *want* to help." I moved my hand to his shoulder to pull him up. "Please tell me. What's happened to this place? Why is it destroyed?"

"It was Razora. She has remained a relentless force. Though she continues to hide, she appears as she wills, making her presence known."

"Is there nothing you can do?"

"We are trying. We have sought the help of other queens, but they are reluctant to come against her."

"And another queen would be able to fight her?"

Levvi sighed. "Well, we are not entirely sure. Glacia's queen holds a lot of power, and Razora is in fact Glacia's queen. The other merqueens, however, are our best bet. But so far, no one has been willing to try, so we do not know."

"What about them?" I gestured around the room to the unicorns.

"The unicorns have agreed to help us, for they have their own cause with Razora."

"And what is that?" I asked, worried and scared for the kind creatures sleeping under the starlight.

"It is believed she holds captive some dear unicorn friends and is using their magic to slow her time. We think it is how she has managed such a long life."

I shook my head at the terrible thought. "But isn't this enough?" I asked, scanning the vast space. "There's so many of them."

Levvi followed my gaze around the pasture. "Their magic is meant to protect and heal. It cannot kill Razora. She does not like it, though, and with so many here by our side, they have lessened her strikes against us."

I turned to Levvi. The hole in my heart was starting to bleed. I swallowed a sour lump. "You need me, huh?" I asked, suddenly feeling sick.

"No," said Levvi with a warm smile. "We do not."

I nodded reluctantly. "Yeah, you do." I exhaled a shaky breath. "This isn't fair," I cried. "How is it fair? How are you not able to fight against such evil? She is not even the real queen. It isn't right!"

"No, it is not fair, but it is the way it is."

"I don't believe that," I said, shaking my head. "There's got to be another way."

"What do you propose, my princess?"

I thought of Peter. "Levvi, we think there's another answer you guys aren't seeing. Is the law written somewhere? Someplace we can read it? Maybe the answer's in there."

"Yes, there is the Tablet Law," he said. He shook his head. "I am sorry to tell you, my princess, but it will do you no good. I have pored over those words countless times. I assure you, you will find nothing new."

"There has to be, though," I said, unwilling to accept this.

"Surely this can't be the end for this beautiful city just because one evil queen decides so. How does she have the right to make that decision? How does she have the power?"

He shook his head doubtfully.

"Please!" I pleaded.

"I suppose it could not hurt," he consented. "Come. I will show you the way."

Levvi led the way down a path of meandering stone corridors. The glowing lavender vial around his neck lit the dark passages just enough so I could see. We walked, twisting and turning in a knot of mazes until at last we came to an end and stopped in front of a stone door, large and grand and intricately carved—a splendid marvel just on its own. Levvi pushed it open.

The room glowed blue. A dim moonlight shimmer flooded the space. But if it was moonlight, it was more sparkly and more magical and so much bluer than the light of any full moon I'd ever witnessed.

I blinked twice at the sight before me, then stood wide-eyed and gaping.

The space was circular, not very big around, but when I looked up, I saw it stretched high like an elevator shaft, extending up for hundreds of feet until at the very top it narrowed and faded into a pinpoint of light.

Covering the walls of the room, all up and down the long length of it, were rows and rows of stone tablets neatly and orderly arranged like library books. Yet unlike library books, the tablets sat floating on invisible shelves.

Everything was blurry and distorted to my eyes because I was looking through a tubular-shaped form of water that filled the center of the room and continued to follow it up as far as I could see. The water floated freely with no walls to contain it, and Levvi crossed under the door and stepped into the liquid sparkles.

He stretched his arms up and kicked. Immediately, his legs became a shimmering silver tail, and he swam up the watery tube, coming to a stop a couple of stories high. I craned my neck to watch as he pulled a tablet from a shelf, stopped the flutter of his tail, and descended back down to the ground. He splashed out of the water and his fins were feet again.

He handed me the dripping tablet. "I hope you find something in here," he said. "For these laws are quite literally set in stone and cannot be changed."

"I hope so, too. Thank you, Levvi." I ran my fingers along the tiny etched script that covered the front and back of the stone. My hope evaporated. The writing was in a strange language I didn't recognize. "It looks like I won't be able to read it after all," I said, handing it back to him.

He pushed the tablet toward me. "Try again," he said. "You might be surprised that you can."

I questioned Levvi with dubious eyes.

He nudged the tablet toward me again. "Try," he repeated.

I looked down at the tablet and once again stared at scroll letters I did not recognize. Then, suddenly, I was connecting their shapes with sounds, and words I understood began to form on the stone. Their meaning became clear. Their sounds I now knew. And in another moment, I was holding a manuscript in a foreign language that was, somehow, that of my own.

"How is this possible?" I asked.

"You are one of us," said Levvi with no falsehood. "And languages tend to come very easily to us."

"My Spanish teacher might disagree with that," I said, astonished, staring at the tablet in my hands.

"This language here," said Levvi, pointing at the pretty etched writing, "it is a part of you. The magic is in you, Ellie."

I paused, thinking about that for a moment.

"So, Levvi?"

"Yes?"

"What would it mean if I were to stay here? Would I never be able to go back?"

He shook his head. "No, I do not ask that of you anymore, Ellie."

"I know," I said. "I'm just . . . I'm just curious if I did decide to stay."

"Yes, it would mean sacrificing much of your life above. As you can see, just a few weeks up in your world, and Glacia has gone on to see decades. Trying to balance the two would be very complicated, to say the least."

"I see," I said. "I still want to help, though. I'm going to be back soon with a plan. I prom—"

A loud *crash* echoed through the hall. I turned to Levvi. "What was that?"

27

We dashed out of the room and ran through a maze of corridors to the sound.

There were footsteps ahead of us and the voice of someone shouting Levvi's name. Starla came around the corner in a sprint. The pretty mermaid ran up to Levvi, embracing him in a hug.

"She's here," cried Starla. "In the entrance hall. I have called on Midnight and the others. We do not know what she wants." Starla then turned to me. "Oh, Ellie! I am very happy to see you." She smiled, but it quickly faded. Her worried gaze lingered on me for a long moment before turning back to Levvi. "What do we do, Levvi? Should we hide her?"

I shook my head at that idea. "No, I'm not hiding. I'm coming."

An anxious breath fluttered over Levvi's lips before he spoke. "She cannot hurt Ellie. Let us go see what she wants."

We crossed under the archway and came into the entrance hall. A large merwoman was standing in a shallow pool in the center of the dark, cavernous room. The lavender light from the glowing water reached up, casting her sharp features in an eerie glow.

As we entered, she turned our way and locked eyes with me.

Razora was unusually tall with long legs that stuck out like sticks behind a high-slitted black dress, wet and slick and clinging tightly to her ribs and over her towering frame. The sleek fabric stopped at her chest to reveal bare, pale-skinned shoulders. Her hair was pulled up into a long braid that fell to her ankles, and long violet tendrils fell from the sides, framing an old but pretty powder-white face. A kiss of crimson colored her lips, and the black that lined the top of her big, dark eyes was sharp and bold against the white canvas. She was strikingly beautiful, but her sharp, penetrating eyes revealed a darkness that was mean and ugly, and it sent shivers down my spine.

Keeping her gaze and her stance locked, she held her arms to her side and twisted her palms up. A beam of light, brilliant and white, switched on, blasting from her palms and shooting a pointed spotlight to the high ceiling above.

The room, quickly filling with sleepy merfolk, sank back in fear at the sight of the luminescent power.

With a flick of her wrist, Razora's palms were down, generating a sparkle of bright light on the pool of water where she stood. The whole place was illuminated as waves of brilliant light reflected on the walls and the ceiling of the cavernous room.

"Good evening, my friends," she shrieked. The room was quiet, and her voice hissed a loud echo in the vast space. She smiled wickedly.

Slowly and deliberately, she raised her hands and the lights to her sides. Her arms tightened stiffly as the light forcefully shot from her palms, sending out destructive laser beams in both directions. She swept her arms up. The laser struck the wall on one side, searing a line in the stone, causing it to break and crumble where it touched. On the other side, it hit the wall made of pure water, breaking through its surface and spilling a forceful fountain into the room. Her wicked smile stretched wide. With her arms reaching high over her head, she flicked her wrist one more time, curling her fingers into a tight fist, and the lights were off.

She lowered her arms, climbed over the edge of the pool, and slowly crept her way forward.

She glided over to us and stopped to pace back and forth in front of Levvi, who had stepped forward, acting as a barrier for Starla and me. Midnight, with his light shining brightly at the tip of his horn, joined his side.

I quickly hid the tablet under my hoodie.

"What are you doing here, Razora?" asked a nervous and frightened Levvi.

Razora smiled slyly. "Oh . . . I just thought it might be a nice night to come pay my good friends in Glacia a visit," she shrieked. Her loud, pitchy voice was icy and sharp. It bounced off the walls of the large room, hitting each of the poor souls standing around like a frosty blast. They shivered with fear.

Veins popped on the back of Levvi's neck. "Razora, get out of here!" he shouted with wretched disdain coming deep from his throat.

"Oh, Levvi," she said, feigning dismay. "Why must you be so rude? I mean you no harm. Truly. You needn't be so harsh."

"So why then have you come tonight?" asked Levvi, sounding exasperated.

"I have come to greet the newcomer," she answered. She looked past Levvi's shoulder, piercing me with her sharp gaze. "Was no one going to introduce us?"

She senselessly scouted the silent room for an answer.

"I am sorry, my dear," she said, circling Levvi to stand before me. "You must excuse their lack of manners. My presence can sometimes be a bit . . . discombobulating." She shot a shrewd wink toward Levvi.

"What is your name, dear?" she asked in a synthetically sweet tone that made my stomach churn.

I was silent as she stood beside me.

"You do not wish to tell me your name? Then perhaps we can play a little guessing game, shall we?" Razora put a finger to her lips and pressed. "Now you tell me if I'm getting close. Is it . . . oh . . . hmm . . . ? I don't know . . ." She feigned ignorance. "Cordelia? Or Ellie, as they may say?"

I flinched.

Her red lips stretched up slyly. "Oh, so that is it." She glared at me maliciously. "You know, I may have heard a little about you, Ellie," she said, pacing in front of me. "Are you not the little princess who comes with the plans to usurp my throne and cast me out forever!" Her voice rose in volume, reverberating loudly around the room, and a thunderous shockwave rippled and shook the floor at her feet.

The merfolk cowered at the sound of it, and I felt pity for them, having lived in fear of this wretched woman for so long. It was enough.

LIGHTS AT MIDNIGHT

Suddenly, there was courage in me I didn't know I had. All the uncertainty, all the worry that plagued me, was gone. And here and now, in this moment, I knew who I was and what I was supposed to do. I stood my ground, staring back at Razora boldly, unflinching this time.

"You need to leave, Razora," I demanded in a hushed whisper. She eyed me contemptuously and took a step back.

"Oh, so the little princess is brave? You think you can come here and start making demands, and I am to bow down to you? Is that it? No, I will not make it so easy, my dear."

"You have no power here, Razora."

"No power!" she laughed mockingly. "Do you not see the crumbling walls? I have all the power of the greatest merqueen. It is only time before all that live here bow to me and worship me as their true queen."

"You will not touch them again," I said. "You no longer have power over these merpeople. They have lived in fear for too long. Your reign is over, Razora."

She laughed. "And what is a little girl like you going to do about it?" Razora stopped in front of me, her jaw tight and clenched, her eyes sharp and focused and matching my hard gaze.

Unwavering, I stared back. "I'm going to ask you to leave," I whispered.

Razora, rigid and still, steamed fiercely in my direction. I kept my gaze locked and steady with hers.

"Go," I said.

She cocked her head and straightened her arms to her sides. Light shot from her palms, shining brightly on the white stone floor and reflecting grim shadows onto her features. "I don't think so," she hissed.

She brought her hands up in an effort to use them against me, but an invisible force within and around me stopped them and blocked the powerful surge of light. It blasted at my protective force field, hitting it with a jolt and causing Razora to lose balance and stumble backward. She looked up at me with frightened eyes. She quickly collected herself and seethed at me viciously, but it was too late; I saw through the thin disguise. She was afraid. She was afraid of *me*.

"*Leave*, Razora!" I roared.

With the bold command, my body came alive. A tingling sensation shot through my nerves and rippled over my skin. It vibrated, pulsed, and thundered through me. The ground beneath me shook with the might of an earthquake, and Razora fell to her knees. She cowered on the floor and glared at me with loathful eyes.

"*Go!*" I yelled.

"This isn't over, little princess." Her words pierced sharply through gritted teeth. "I will be back!" She shot up and dashed across the room. She jumped into the wall of water, turning into a fluttering mermaid with a glistening black tail. She swam hastily out of sight, disappearing into the dark abyss beyond.

The room exploded with happy cheers and laughter. The celebration boomed around the large space, and words of praise for my own name echoed in my ear.

I looked around at their happy faces and felt a dreadful surge of guilt rise inside me. Levvi gazed back at me with sympathetic eyes, and I knew that he knew.

"Quiet, everyone," he said. The crowd ignored his request and continued its happy celebration. "Quiet!" he yelled, his voice echoing loudly across the expanse. The laughter ceased, and all eyes fell upon him. "She is not staying."

In a reversal of emotions, their grinning faces turned down, and the crowd bellowed in anger. They turned to me.

"You are leaving us? But you can't," said an elderly merlady.

I peered around the room at their angry and pitiful faces. They stared back, waiting for an answer.

"I'm sorry, but I can't stay," I said.

"What? But you can't leave," the merlady added. The crowd echoed its disapproval.

"This is not my life," I said. "My life is at home with my family—with Peter."

"Peter? Who is this Peter?" a large merman called out.

"Never mind," I said. "It doesn't matter, but I will help you. I won't leave you to fight her alone. Please trust me. I will be back."

I looked to Levvi. "Go," he said.

I grasped the tablet tightly and headed toward the elevator. The crowd roared behind me as I ascended.

28

An alarm buzzed and beeped loudly in my ear. I fumbled around for my phone. I smacked my hand on something hard but couldn't find the source of the detestable tone. I opened my eyes. My head was resting on my desk, not my pillow. I peeled my face off the smooth surface.

The dim glow of my phone's alarm was in front of me. I reached to shut it off. My phone was sitting on top of the tablet. I glared at the solid stone block with irritation.

After returning home, I stayed up all night, trying to work out the meaning of the words on the surface.

I hadn't gotten very far. It seemed as though Levvi might have been right all along.

The writing had mentioned the heir, the queen, the bloodline, but nothing else as far as I could tell. There was nothing that gave me any clues on how to defeat Razora. But I was still hoping there was something my tired brain wasn't seeing. I was eager to get it to Peter so he could help me figure it all out.

I got up and dressed for school, then took the stone tablet and placed it in my backpack right next to my math book. There really was no need to hide it. I could take it downstairs with me, waving it like a flag, and Dad and Millie would think nothing of it.

They'd assume I got it online or something. At most, they might think it was a replica of some kind. I knew they would never even consider the possibility that it was an ancient artifact from a magical mermaid land. In fact, I was sure I could tell them the exact truth as to where I got it and they still wouldn't bat an eye.

This was sort of a relief and sort of frustrating at the same time. It meant I could never share with them the biggest thing that ever happened to me—thank God I had Peter.

"Coffee?" questioned Dad, seeing me pour a cup for myself.

"Yeah, is that okay? I'm really tired today. I had a headache last night and didn't sleep much." I was only distorting the truth a little.

"You feeling better this morning?" he asked, his eyes narrow with concern.

"Yeah," I said. "I'm okay. Just tired."

I took the coffee and my bowl of cereal over to the island to sit next to Dad.

"I'm going to hang out with Peter after school today," I said.

I shoved a spoonful of cereal into my mouth, chewing as quickly as I could. I was eager to get this school day over with so I could talk to Peter.

Dad put his coffee down. "I don't know, Ellie. Don't you think you've been hanging out with that boy a little too much?"

"He's my friend."

"Yeah, I know. But maybe it's about time you give Peter a break and call up one of the girls," he suggested.

I frowned at that idea. "I see them at school every day, Dad."

"I know. I just worry about you, Ellie. You've got to be careful around boys." He raised his cup to take a sip and looked at me sternly from behind the brim.

"Dad," I said, meeting his gaze. "I don't have to be careful around Peter."

"No?" He raised an eyebrow at me.

"No." I shook my head, keeping steady eyes on his. "Trust me."

Dad eyed me hesitantly for a second, then nodded. "All right," he said. "Still. Be smart."

Ouch. His words cut deep. I knew how much Peter would agree with that sentiment, and he would be the one to tell Dad I *wasn't* being so smart these days.

There was a loud knock at the door. Dad and I turned our heads.

"Hello!" a woman's voice called from outside.

Dad got up.

"Hello, sir, I'm sorry to bother you. Are you Ellie's father?"

I recognized the voice and rushed to the door. "Mrs. Evans?"

A worried and distraught woman stood in front of us. She was wearing a house robe and had her arms wrapped tightly around her waist to keep it closed. Her hair was a frantic mess, and her face was streaked with tears that smeared yesterday's makeup. "Ellie, is Peter here?" she asked. She was shaking.

My heart sank. "No, Mrs. Evans." She was scaring me. "No. Why? Where is he?" I desperately searched her face for an answer.

"He's not at home," she cried. "He was really upset when you left yesterday. He stayed in his room all night, and when I went to check on him this morning . . ." She craned her neck around me to see inside. "He's really not here? I thought . . ." She began to sob. "Oh God, I don't know where else to check."

It took me only a second. I looked to the woods behind Mrs. Evans and knew.

"Oh, Peter," I whispered to myself. *What have you done?* I turned back to Dad and Mrs. Evans. There was no time to explain. I grabbed my jacket from the hook near the door. "I might know where he is," I said. "Just wait here."

I ran past them and headed toward the trails.

"Ellie, get back here!" hollered Dad.

I kept running. I had to be quick. Every second meant . . . *forever. Oh no.* If Peter was in Glacia, how long had it been?

I reached the lake and waded through the water. I lowered my locket and went down.

The lobby was brightly lit, the water outside blue and tranquil with the new day, but there was no one in sight. "Levvi!" I shouted to the empty room.

I searched around, hoping I would see someone—anyone. I didn't know where to go. It would be impossible to find Midnight's enclosure. The passages had been so dark, and I didn't remember how I got there.

"Levvi!" I shouted again.

I started toward the archway in the back but stopped short. There was a shadow swimming in the water outside. Someone was out there, a dark figure in the distance. I thought it was a mermaid.

I could barely make out the silhouette of her tail fin, but I was sure that was what I saw. If only I could get her attention, she could help me.

I walked over to the arched doorway leading out to the sea. I leaned over the river of water that flowed from the opening and tried to yell through the door.

"Hey!" I called to the mermaid. She didn't respond and continued to swim away from me. "Hello!" I called again, but she faded into the darkness.

It was no use.

I took a deep breath and tried to think. My only option was to look for Midnight or anyone else that might be down inside the tunnels.

I turned to go.

My foot caught on a bumpy stone that stuck out near the edge of the water, and I was knocked off balance. I flailed my arms, grasping at air, trying impossibly to catch myself.

I fell.

With a dreadful splash, I was in the water.

It was icy and rough. The current was strong near the door, and it pulled and dragged me with it. The water splashed over my head and I went under. I waved my arms frantically and kicked hard against the force, but I was not strong enough. I struggled to remove my heavy, water-laden jacket. I tried again with freed arms, but it was useless. The current pulled on me and I was powerless to stop it. It grabbed hold, fierce and strong, and swept me up and out toward the open sea.

No! my soul cried. *I can't go out there!*

I tried one last time and gave it my all, but it was no use, and in mere seconds, I was on the other side of the wall, in the underwater world outside.

I kicked again and tried to swim back, but the current swept me away, pushing me farther out. I tried once more, but I didn't have the strength to fight against it.

I was trapped.

I scanned the bright room in front of me. No one was there to help.

This is it, I thought. I was going to die in an underwater mermaid lair. *My dad. Oh, my poor dad.* Would they tell him?

My lungs ached, and dark spots clouded my vision.

Oh, the pain . . .

I couldn't hold my breath any longer, and I knew it was time.

Bye, beautiful world.

I took a long, deep, involuntary inhale. My mouth and throat filled with salty water . . . but my lungs were clear, and I breathed.

I breathed!

Glorious life-giving bubbles of oxygen filled my lungs, and the pain that had been there began to melt away. I took another breath and started to cry.

It was water, yes, but somehow, it didn't matter.

A second later, a strange tingling sensation surged through my body. It started in my chest and reached down to the tip of my toes, an electrical signal traveling through my nerves. It lingered and pulsed in spasms at my feet. I peered down.

There had been a change.

I squinted and stared hard, certain my blurry, watery eyes were distorting the image. But no. *My legs!* They were gone and had been replaced with a shimmery navy-blue tail.

I smiled gleefully—I was a mermaid.

I was a mermaid!

I kicked and twirled in the water to try and get a better look and found I glided through it with ease. I fluttered my tail again and swam around in circles.

"Woo hoo!" I screamed, my voice coming out as a strange gurgling sound.

I swam farther out into the abyss, reveling in excitement. I wanted to see how fast I could go and quickly realized I was a jet soaring through a water-sky, leaving a contrail of bubbles in my wake.

Amazing!

Reluctantly, I turned back.

Peter.

I needed to focus.

That was when I saw it. For the first time, I was looking at the city of Glacia from the outside, and I marveled at the sight.

What stood before me was a magnificent and grand white stone castle carved into the side of a rocky seamount. It stretched high with several cylindrical towers that reached up and pierced through the icy blue waters. The open window of the entrance hall glowed brightly, illuminating the bubbly waters around it and casting the whole thing in a sparkling spotlight. It was a wondrous sight that took my breath away.

A multitude of windows was scattered about the dazzling surface. The windows were dark, all except for a glowing row of them that curved around at the top of one of the taller towers. I swam back to the castle, weaving in and out of the large stone structure until I reached the light. I crouched under one of the open windows and carefully peeked inside, hiding myself from view.

Through a curtain of raining water, I peered into a room I recognized. It was the same room I had been in before—the dome with a matching round pool in its center and where we met on our first trip to Glacia. And like before, there was a meeting taking place.

Dozens of merfolk crowded around inside. They were arguing. I listened carefully, straining to hear their muffled voices through the water. But their voices were songs again. I didn't understand . . . not at first. I continued to listen, and like the words on the tablet before, the meanings of the strange melodious language began to become clear in my mind. It took only a few seconds, and I was understanding and listening in secret beside the window.

"We will let him go," demanded a male voice. It was Levvi. He was standing near the pool in front of the crowd.

"We will *not*," bellowed another merman in a low baritone voice. He was the same large merman who I had spoken with—just last night. But it hadn't been last night for them, had it?

"This will not work. You fools!" said Levvi. "What were you thinking? Release him now! You are all but sealing our fate with this move."

"It is our last hope, Levvi. We have tried rallying forces from the other mercities. No one will join our side. They are too afraid. They do not want to come under Razora's wrath. They have seen the destruction she can cause.

"The princess has forced our hands and now we wait. It is far better than doing nothing. Do you see what doing nothing has done to our city? We are shrinking! It is only a matter of time before they all leave. And we will be destroyed just as Razora wants."

"He has already been here too long. You know that, Strom!" Levvi's voice shook. "And you have hidden this from Starla and me. Do we not consult the council anymore when making such fatal decisions?"

"The council was informed," said a shrill female. "It was voted upon."

"We took no part in this vote," a soft voice said, and Starla rose to stand beside Levvi.

"What can I say?" said the shrill female. "If you were not part of the meeting, then it cannot be our fault."

"But you knew we were attending to matters outside the city!" yelled Levvi.

"We needed a foolproof plan to get her back," said the large merman named Strom. "She is likely on her way right now as we speak. And besides, it's not like we went out of our way to capture him. He came to us."

"He's just a boy," pleaded Levvi.

At those words, I felt the burning sting of fury like I had never known. There was no containing it. It bubbled and boiled, shooting lava painfully up to scorch my throat, and the ashy taste it left in my mouth was foul.

They had Peter!

I made a move to pull myself through the window. I would get Peter and we were going. We would leave this place forever.

My fingers grasped at the window frame. I pushed up onto the ledge, pulling my body through. Just as I managed a sitting position on the stone sill, a large bony hand reached around my waist and grasped me tightly, dragging me back into the water.

"Levvi!" I yelled. My voice escaped just before I was completely immersed again. Levvi looked my way, but it was too late.

The hand dragged me up along the length of a tall tower. I tried to scream, but my words were gurgles now. I writhed and kicked, but like the current before, this hand was too strong. It pulled me higher and higher up the side of the tower. A long tendril of violet hair floated in front of my eyes, and I knew who it was that had captured me.

Razora jetted up to a lone window at the top of a high tower. She threw me at the water-paned glass, and I came crashing down onto a wet stone floor. I slid across the slippery surface, slamming my head into a wall before stopping.

Ouch! Pain throbbed where it hit. I inhaled the air around me and felt the change. The mermaid tail had disappeared, and my wet denim legs were back.

I glanced around the room. It was cold and dark, like a dungeon in the watery sky. I could faintly make out a circular stone wall in front of me. The floor was covered in a layer of shallow water, and the dark stone walls held on to the chill. A shiver ran through me, but I wasn't sure if it was the cold or the *fear* that had me shaking.

The wall I had hit was smooth glass. I pressed myself against it, keeping my eyes locked on the window I had come through. Long bony fingers clawed through the water and wrapped around the edge of the stone frame.

Razora pulled herself in.

29

The tall mermaid took slow, bony steps, sloshing through the water toward me. I stared up at her from the wet floor, helpless and weak.

"Oh, Ellie, I thought that was you," she oozed sweetly. A pleased smile stretched her lips thin and wide. The pointed ends directed me to vicious and scheming eyes that glowered in my direction. "It's so very nice to see you again. And what an exciting time, with you getting your tail and all. It seems you are becoming quite the little mermaid, aren't you?"

She stopped in front of me, fixing her evil eyes on mine. I tried to move away, but pain shot through my head again. I winced.

"Are you hurt, dear? I am oh so sorry," she said with mock sympathy. "It really is a shame that it had to come to this, my child."

"Razora, please," I said weakly. I had no fight in me this time. Whatever power that was in me before was gone. "I am not a threat to you. Just let me go."

"Let you go?" She cocked her head.

"Yes," I cried.

"Now why would I do that?"

"I just want to get out of here. I won't come back. I promise." Then I whispered a promise to myself. "I'm never coming back."

Razora studied me with curiosity. "Hmm . . . well, I may be inclined to believe you. After all, I can understand why you might feel at odds with these silly merfolk." She laughed. "I agree they have been quite foolish, though I think, this time, their foolhearted act is going to prove quite beneficial to me."

Her evil eyes brightened, then darted sideways as a door boomed open.

In stormed Levvi and Midnight, accompanied by a dozen more merfolk at their heels. Midnight's light beamed brightly from his horn. It lit the room, reflecting off the shiny, wet walls.

Starla broke from the group and ran to my side. She helped me off the watery floor, and we stood trembling together in front of Razora.

Razora eyed the newcomers with glee. "Welcome, Levvi and friends," she said. "We were just discussing your generosity, for you have been so kind as to wrap up this sweet gift for me." She waved her arms and gestured behind me.

I turned around.

The light from Midnight's horn shone brightly around the room, lighting the wall that I had been pressed against. I took a step back.

The smooth glass wall was just one side of a dark and massive glass cube that sat in the center of the circular room.

I turned questioning eyes to Razora, then to Levvi. His grief-stricken eyes met mine with sorrow.

"What's going on, Levvi? Where's Peter?"

Levvi was quiet. I silently beseeched Starla by my side. Neither of them answered.

"Tell her," said Razora. "Or should I?"

Levvi looked at me with sad eyes. "He is here," he said finally.

"Here?" I twisted, searching for Peter. He was nowhere among the group of merfolk that had arrived. "Where?" I asked desperately. He wasn't answering quickly enough. "Where is Peter, Levvi?"

Then Levvi nodded to the box behind me, and the realization hit—*it was a cage.*

"Is he in there?" I asked.

Levvi nodded.

"Let him out!"

"I do not think that would be wise, my princess."

My patience broke. "I am not your princess!" I seethed. I looked around at the merfolk in the room. "You *will* let him go!"

I glared at them, my eyes hot with tears. No one moved. I stared at them blankly. "Have you really captured him?" They didn't answer. "I am not believing this," I said, shaking my head. "I have been wrestling with whether or not to come here. I do not owe you anything, yet I had all the desire in my heart to help you, and now I don't know why." My eyes were hard with disbelief. "Release him!" I demanded. "Now!"

Levvi stepped forward—tears streamed down his face.

"I would, Ellie," he whispered. "But I do not think we should right now." He glanced at Razora in fear and then back to the prison that held Peter.

Razora stepped forward. "Oh, come now," she said. "Let's let him out, shall we?"

She strode over to the wall and pressed an invisible button. A dim glow circled around her finger. The cube lit brightly, and the insides behind the clear glass were revealed.

It was a cell, a glass room with a single bed in the center, and from under a blanket, Peter's dirt-clad sneakers dangled off the end of the mattress.

"Peter!" I screamed.

He didn't stir.

"Open this at once!" I demanded.

"Of course," said Razora. She pressed the button again, and a door turned to vapor in front of me. Water splashed into the room, flooding the floor of the prison.

I rushed to Peter's side. "Peter!" I cried. I tugged at his shirt, but there was no response. "What's wrong with him? What did you do?"

Levvi stepped into the room and stood beside me.

"The room has the magic to pause," said Levvi. "It was suggested so too much time did not pass for him here."

"How long has he been here?"

Levvi hesitated. "He has been here for nearly eight months."

I gasped. "Eight months?"

Levvi knelt beside me. "I was not aware of it, Ellie. I promise," he whispered.

"Will he be okay?" Peter was pale and his eyes were dusty circles.

"I do not know, for he has been a long time in two worlds. I think so, though."

"Why isn't he moving?"

"It will take a moment for him to wake up," said Levvi.

I put my hand on Peter's forehead. His head shifted under my touch.

"Peter," I whispered. He stirred again.

"Ellie?" He spoke in a stupor.

"Yeah, I'm here. It's okay. We're going to go home. It's going to be al—"

A hand was tapping my shoulder. I turned to Levvi, who was trying to get my attention. Behind us, he fixed scared eyes on Razora, who was standing at the entrance of the enclosure.

I swiftly moved to the door, blocking her way. "Don't you dare!" I raged.

Suddenly, there was power running through my veins again. Where it was coming from and why it was there, I didn't know. But it was a part of me—natural, real, and all mine. And a steady courage, intermixed with this power, turned my resolve to iron; she would be no match for me now. "You stay away from him," I demanded.

With the rise of my voice, the ground vibrated and small waves rippled in the water beneath us. Razora felt it, too, and took a step back. A tinge of fear swept across her pale face, turning it ashen and dry, but she was quick and pulled the mask back up.

"Oh!" she said sweetly, giving no indication she feared anything at all. "Do we have ourselves a little boyfriend here?"

She peered over my shoulder and into the room. I stood my ground in front of the door.

"You leave him *alone*!" I roared. Again, the floor rumbled—stronger this time—and the water splashed violently, hitting the walls with heavy waves. "Get out of here, Razora!" I pointed at the window she had crawled through.

She seethed and took another step back, sneering at me ferociously. "Why must you always be in my way?" she hissed.

"I gave you a chance to let me go," I shot back at her. "This was your choice."

"So you have decided now to stay?" She tilted her head in confusion. "Even after all they have done?"

"They are acting out of fear, Razora. That is all your power brings, fear and destruction. Even the purest of hearts struggle against it. How dare you lead them astray! I won't stand by and watch it any longer!"

Razora stared at me, bewildered. She cocked her head again, and now sprinkled with the hatred, a look of pity adorned her face. "Oh, Ellie. But surely you must know by now," she said.

"Know what?" I asked.

She sighed wearily and continued. "That the seed I watered was planted long before me."

I peered at her, puzzled.

"Yes, these merfolk hide it well, but alas, their true colors are coming to light." She stopped to glance around the room. "For this isn't the first time that these merfolk of Glacia are finding it difficult to accept a human, especially these human boys that, oh so easily, steal our mermaid hearts. Sadly, it is history repeating itself." She cast her eyes down disappointedly and shook her head.

"What do you mean, Razora?" I asked. Her efforts to reel me in had worked, and I bit at the line with piqued interest.

"Ah . . . so it is what I thought. You have not been informed of their true history, have you?"

I looked to Levvi, who met my eyes with hesitation. His gaze faltered and fell to his feet.

"Time for a quick history lesson, I suppose," said Razora. "So where should I start? How about from the time poor Queen Leira was cast out of her city for mere love? That seems like a good place to begin. Don't you think, Levvi?" She shot a mocking smile toward Levvi, who remained quiet and sullen.

"Cast out?" I asked. "I thought she left."

Razora laughed. "Oh, that is the story they would have told, isn't it? But no." She paused and smiled up at the room gleefully. She turned back to me with delighted eyes. "I'd be happy to clear things up a bit," she said. "Let me tell you how I remember the events.

"Back when I lived here in Glacia, as a young mermaid not much older than you are, I had a best friend. Her name was Leira.

"Leira was a loyal and devoted friend and princess and became a great queen who loved her city. Her heart was pure—the purest of them all—and it was no surprise she easily loved humans as though they were our equals. She, in fact, found humans and the world above fascinating and spent much of her time fixated on them."

Razora's eyes turned down as she continued.

"I suffered heartache when she fell in love with the man that lived above, for I loved Leira. But I learned to accept it because I saw that she was happy. But *they* could not.

"The fools cast him out of the city, despite her pleading, despite her loyalty.

"Leira remained in Glacia, but she was heartbroken and torn and was never the same after that day. She tried her best to be a devoted queen, but with a broken and distraught soul, she found it hard to continue with her duties.

"The fools of Glacia would not have it. Carrying out their greatest mistake, they cast out their weak and vulnerable queen, banishing her to the shore, demanding she never return. And with heartache and despair, poor Leira obliged. She stayed away as they requested and built her home and life above—apart from us all."

Razora stopped and looked up, wiping a lone tear from her eye. And for a split second, the sad young mermaid from the past was standing before me. She glared at me, and her eyes devolved back to darkness, back to the present-day evil she had let herself become.

"Did they not tell you this part?" she asked. Her voice held on to the pain and it came out faint with markings of her grief—I felt pity for her.

I stared at the merfolk standing around in the room, then turned to Levvi, who had taken his place beside me at the door. His eyes met mine with trepidation.

"Is this true?" I asked.

"What she says is true," he said. "We were scared and acted out of fear. I am sorry I have kept this from you, Ellie. It is part of our shameful past, and I only wanted to forget it."

"You only wanted to hide it from me." I shook my head at him. "I needed to know this, Levvi. You can't run from your past. Look what's happened here."

Levvi nodded solemnly.

Razora turned dark eyes to him. "So, I am curious, Levvi," she said. "What was the plan here? Were you to take this boy, forever holding him hostage so she can be your little princess?"

LIGHTS AT MIDNIGHT

A small and distraught Levvi left her unanswered as he studied the ground at his feet. "It seems they are bigger fools than even I realized, my dear," Razora said to me. "Oh, such fools." She smiled wickedly. "Do you really not see the error in your plan here?"

The room was silent.

Razora gazed upon Levvi with pity and disdain. "I suppose I will go on," she said, turning back to me and continuing her story. "And so, you see . . . these fools cast out their own queen. It wasn't long after that they realized the sheer folly of their actions, for in those days our own Tablet Laws were hidden away for only the most noble to read. It had been many years since anyone had looked upon them, so in fairness, the poor fools of Glacia had no way of knowing. No one knew what the true consequences of our actions would be. But we soon found out, didn't we?"

She sneered at the room, then continued. "Once Leira was gone, they tried to exalt others to the throne as queen, but it was no use. When Leira left, she took with her the power she possessed as queen, and there was no way to transfer that power to another."

"Then how is it that you have power?" I asked.

"I am getting to that part, my dear," she said impatiently. "You see, there is one other way to gain the power of a queen . . ." She trailed off and looked at the quiet room, which stared back, dumbfounded. "It was never recorded or known because the ancient magic was lost to us. In fact, it was my dear Leira who made the discovery.

"When Leira was cast out, we remained dear friends. She confided in me about her misery and heartache over losing her city. It was she herself who realized that as the true queen she could bestow the power of the queen to another. And so, she did. She handed her power to me . . . so I could rule this city in greatness, since she could not."

I searched Levvi's shaken eyes. "Did you know about this?" I asked.

He shook his head. "No, Ellie. We did not. Queen Leira never spoke of this."

I turned back to Razora. "So that's it?" I cried, astounded. "That's all it takes? Leira gives you permission and you can destroy everything?"

"Well, no," said Razora with a sinister grin. "And this is the best part . . . and it was never written in the laws because it never needed to be, for it is something that is inherent in all merprincesses." She smiled cunningly. "I worked it out for myself when I saw just how weak and vulnerable my poor Leira had become when her love was so cruelly torn from her. You see, my dear princess, a true queen—even an heir from the purest of bloodlines such as yourself—has one more responsibility before she can gain the power of an almighty merqueen."

I stared at Razora, confused. "And what is that?" I asked.

"The queen alone is not powerful enough to rule a city," continued Razora. "No, there is one other thing that is needed, and it resides in the heart of every princess—it is the ability to love. Binding love with the power of the merqueen is what makes her mighty and strong.

"It is not just the heir's blood but her *love* that gives her power. This great city had all of that, but they removed Leira and, with her, the power of her love. The one thing keeping us strong." She paused and stared at me coldly.

The room was quiet.

"I don't understand, Razora," I said, breaking the silence. "If love is needed, how is it you have power? You do not love anything!"

"I loved Leira!" she shouted, throwing a reproachful glare at me.

"You didn't love her. She wouldn't have wanted this!"

Razora's gaze hardened on me. "Don't presume to know me, my child," she spat. Her dark eyes filled with tears. "I loved her . . . till her dying day." She blinked, and the tears splashed down her cheeks. She took a deep breath and sucked them up. "But my love was never enough for Leira."

I stared back at her, into cold eyes and into a broken soul that was even colder and darker. "Razora, any love you may have had for Leira is gone." I stood, perplexed. How could someone so cold profess to love? How did Razora have any power with a heart too icy for something so warm? Where exactly were her powers coming from?

Her eyes twitched, and in them burned a hunger, a thirst for something. For something she loved. Something she craved.

"It is just the power and control and fear that you love," I said. "And it is an evil love that only destroys. It will cause this city to crumble. Is that what you want?"

"Yes!" she hissed. "I want them to pay for their actions!"

"No!" I yelled back at her. "I won't let you hurt them anymore!"

"Yes, I know that, dear. You will always be in my way!" she seethed savagely. "And regretfully, I cannot kill you, for as the true heir, you have power that surpasses mine, and hand in hand with love, that power cannot be defeated." She glowered at me and shook with a heavy breath that steamed from her nose.

There was a scuffle behind me, and I turned. Peter was making a futile attempt to get up. He fell weakly back to the mattress.

"Ellie," he called to me in a cracked whisper.

He made another effort to prop himself onto his elbow. I wanted to go to him, but I dared not take my attention off Razora.

"Hold on, Peter, I—"

"Ellie," he said, cutting me off.

"What?" I asked. I quickly turned to look at him and met frightened eyes. He was scared of something. He tried to speak, but his words were raspy and weak.

Scared and unsure, I turned back to Razora.

Like a prowling bear, she paced in front of the room, eyeing Peter inside. She turned her dark eyes back to me. "You, as the rightful heiress, have always been a lingering threat to me. You and your mother. Leira's whole bloodline . . . up there . . . just waiting and threatening to come back and take it all away. Your mother was hidden well, so I had no choice but to wait. And so I have waited all these long years, frozen in time, for the return of the princess who would come and challenge me." She stared at me coldly. "Your return, Ellie . . . just like I planned."

"My return? You knew I was coming?"

She smiled wickedly. "I might have known a little something, my dear." She paused and let out a contemptuous laugh. "Oh, poor Leira was so ashamed of what she did, so ashamed of me, so willing to turn on me and forget me, and oh so willing to help these stupid fools bring you . . . right to me. All it took was a few well-placed jabs on my part, and they went crawling to her." Razora smiled at me, looking victorious. "And now, once I take care of you, this city will be all mine to crush and destroy."

"But you're forgetting something, Razora," I said. "You can't beat me."

"Ellie . . ." It was Peter again. I twisted my neck to look at him. "Ellie . . . no . . . She's . . . gonna . . ." His raspy voice broke, and he fell back to the bed.

"What?" I mouthed.

"Ah, it is true," said Razora, paying Peter no mind. I turned back to her dark eyes. "I cannot beat you, for you are the true heir and true queen, and combined with the power of true love, I could never defeat you."

She winked at me. There was a sparkle in her eyes, and a look of triumph flashed across her face. With a vicious sneer, she hissed, "Let's take care of that, shall we?"

Razora grabbed at the top of her long braid. She pulled from her hair a short-pointed unicorn's horn. It was broken and jagged at the base and sharp like a needle at the tip. She eyed the inside of the cage where Peter lay.

My heart cried.

"No!" I screamed. I tried to stop her, but she was too quick. Razora pitched the horn over my head and it soared into the room behind me.

Everything slowed.

I watched the pointy dagger sail toward Peter, who had managed to prop himself up into a sitting position on the cot. His sunken face turned to horror as he noticed the incoming missile heading straight his way. I watched as it pierced down, plunging into his heart, and I watched as he fell back to the mattress one last time.

I watched. But that wasn't what I saw—*it couldn't be.*

"Peter!" I screamed.

I sloshed through the water to Peter's side.

Blood soaked his blue shirt, turning it an ugly violet. He wasn't moving. His arms dangled limply over the sides of the small cot. "Peter!" I cried again. "Somebody help him! He's hurt!"

Levvi was by my side, but he did nothing.

"Levvi, help him," I cried. The merman remained still and quiet.

I yanked on Peter's arm to try to get him to wake up. "It's going to be okay, Peter," I said. "We are going to get out of here. You were right. This was stupid. I should have listened to you." I pressed my lips to his. "I'm so sorry," I whispered.

I laid my face on his chest. It did not heave with the intake of breath and there was no heart silently pounding inside. "No," I cried. "Peter, please. Please. You can't leave me."

Hopeless tears streamed down my face.

I closed my eyes.

I fell into a world . . . dark and quiet. I lingered there, where everything was cold, where everything was distant. Time was no more, for it did not matter.

Nothing mattered now.

"Ellie."

A voice broke the silence.

"Ellie."

Someone was whispering my name.

I stayed where I was in my dark, cold space.

"Ellie," it called again. Levvi's voice . . . somewhere in the distance.

A hand was on my shoulder.

"Ellie," he said softly into my ear.

I opened my eyes. My face was sticky and wet from tears and from the blood on Peter's shirt. I kept my head down, resting it on his lifeless body. I stared transfixed at the horn protruding from his chest, just inches from my nose. It was a silvery blue, and though broken and detached from its poor owner, it remained a treasure that glimmered in the light.

I pulled the horn from Peter's inert body.

LIGHTS AT MIDNIGHT

I turned with wet, blurry eyes to Razora, who had entered the room and now stood towering over me. "Why, Razora?" I cried.

"Because you are no threat with a broken heart," she said, her voice quivering with rage. "You cannot rule if you do not love. And now that that has been taken care of, I will finish you off for good!"

She reached down and grabbed me by the shoulders. Her bony fingers wrapped tightly around my arms, digging sharp claws into my skin. She lifted me easily off the ground, bringing me up and level with her eyes. She held tight, staring ferociously into mine. She didn't speak, and the room was silent except for the sound of water dripping down the ends of my shoes, splashing onto the flooded floor below.

I stared back at her dark, lonely eyes and realized I felt nothing but pity for the wretched soul in front of me. "You were once just one of them," I said.

She cocked her head back and eyed me suspiciously. This hadn't been the response she was expecting.

"I was never a fool like them," she sneered.

"You are, though, Razora," I said. "Don't you see?"

Her eyes narrowed in thought, but she didn't answer. It didn't surprise me. This was something she could never understand.

"Your view of love is very narrow, Razora," I said. "You have let the vengeance you seek harden your heart. And in doing so, it has shriveled to nothing."

My voice came out shaking through my chattering teeth. Whether they trembled because I was cold or scared or sad, I couldn't tell. I was all of those things, but none of it mattered now.

I stared into Razora's eyes, seeking a burner that might still be alight. There was only darkness. "You don't have the capacity for love anymore, so you couldn't see beyond what you think you know. And for that I am sorry." I turned my head to look at Peter but only managed a glimpse of his dirty sneakers. "I'm really sorry," I whispered to him, and tears began to fall from my eyes again.

"I think we've had enough of that, dearie," shrieked Razora, throwing me down. I fell with a splash to the floor. "Now it's time to take care of my final threat."

She stepped forward and hovered over me like a lion. She reached down and grasped at the collar of my shirt, pulling me up with one hand, and with the other, she reached long fingers down the length of my arm. She found the horn I still carried and pulled it from my weak grip. She raised it to my throat and stared at me hard, her eyes wicked with intent.

"Goodbye, my princess," she sneered. With a jerk of her wrist, she pulled back just a little and made to thrust forward with the sharp point of the horn.

In a flash of a second, I felt it. It had been there all along—I knew that now. But Razora did not.

Like a bolt of electricity, a power surged through me. It ignited in my bones and pulsed across my skin. In an instant, I was no longer cold, I was no longer scared, and I was no longer weak.

In quick succession, I raised my hand, grabbed at the horn, and turned it around on Razora.

"You are the fool, Razora," I said. I sniffed and turned to peer out into the room where the merfolk stood watching. My heart ached for them, so pitiful and ridden with fear. "You have no idea what love is, Razora. If you ever did, you have forgotten."

I turned my head toward Peter, then back to Razora, who met me with frightened eyes. Tears poured down my face. "And love does not simply die with a person!" I cried angrily.

Aghast, Razora gaped at me. She tried to grab at the horn again, but it was tight and secure in my grip. I shot my hand forward and let out a loud scream. I plunged the point deep into her stomach. Her eyes bulged with pain and shock.

She dropped me from her arms, and I stood in the water, holding onto her. "It's over, Razora," I said with sad tears.

With one more surge, the power inside me escaped through my hand and ran through the horn and out into Razora's body. She convulsed and shook beneath my arms. Her beetle eyes bulged once more. Then they settled into a lifeless stare. I let go, and she fell on her back and splashed down into the water. A river of red streamed from her body.

She was dead.

31

With the splash of Razora's dead body, a wave of jubilance rose around the room. The sound reverberated off the stone walls and echoed a joyous song that fell, muffled, on my ears.

To me, this was a distant memory in some other life . . . in some other universe. I stared at their smiling faces and knew I was happy for them, but I felt nothing.

Levvi walked to stand beside me and put his hand on my shoulder. I let his arm fall as I turned back to Peter's side. I would go back to my quiet world now . . . where all was still.

I sat on the cot beside Peter and took his cold hand in mine and cried. I stared at his blank face and was hollow. A deep gouge in my heart left an emptiness there. An emptiness that could never be filled, because it was the space that had grown for him, and he was gone. *Where are you, Peter?*

A crushing weight pressed down on me and I folded over onto Peter's lifeless body and sobbed.

The room around me grew quiet. The only sound that remained

in the cold, echoey space was the sound of my weeping. But the hush lasted for only a moment, when again the crowded room stirred with joy. The joyous sound rose in volume and beckoned me to look up.

The room of merfolk was gasping in awe at something, a look of wonder spreading across each of their faces. I followed their gazes to the window and to the outside sea.

A bright light shone through the opening, and the luminescent water, pure and still outside, sparkled and bubbled.

Then the source of the light was revealed as, one by one, small glowing orbs floated into view. They drifted through the water and past the window and floated like fireflies into the room. They streamed in by the hundreds, a dazzling diamond necklace that dangled in the air and floated toward the enclosure where I sat beside Peter.

Then, in succession, the individual lights floated down to touch his skin. Their warmth fell over me as they passed by—pleasant and sweet like sunshine kissing your skin on a cold winter's day. They landed softly, starting at his head, then moving down his body. They filled in the spaces until every inch of him was covered in sparkling light.

I moved to stand beside the bed. I stared in awe at the form of Peter's body, now covered in light from head to toe.

The lights merged and grew brighter. As they did, they began to sing. A lovely soft, ambient sound, pure and sweet, poured from their midst. Tears streamed down my face as I listened to the soothing melody. They sang until their song was finished, then they faded and turned off. There was one that remained. It rose in front of me and landed on the tip of my nose. It lingered for a second, then pulsed with a bright light before it, too, turned off and was gone.

There was an instant sense of comfort, and I looked down. My shirt and my jeans, where they were not touching the water, were dry. They were warm, with freshly laundered softness, and all the aches in my body had been dissolved.

My eyes fell on Peter. A seed of hope sprouted within me. I squinted in disbelief.

His skin was pink again. His shirt was untarnished. I placed my hand on his chest where the wound had been. There was no blood. I lifted his shirt to see that his wound had healed. There was no scar or redness to mark the horror. I folded the fabric back down and stared at his blushed cheeks. And then my eyes moved to his, and his opened.

"Peter!" I screamed.

He blinked at me. "Ellie," he said. There was a slight rasp in his voice, but he was speaking. *He was speaking!*

I covered my gaping mouth, staring in disbelief at his beautiful eyes gazing back at me.

I moved my hand to touch his face, so warm and soft. "Oh my god," I cried, bending low on the bed to hug him. I tucked my fingers under his arms and held on. He was oh so warm, and his heart drummed steady and strong inside his chest. I held on, not wanting to let go, not wanting to wake up from this wonderful dream.

"Ellie." Peter squirmed under me.

I pulled myself off and stared at him, happy tears streaming from my eyes.

"What happened?" he asked.

"You're okay," I said, nodding and smiling and still crying. "You're going to be okay."

I looked to my side and out into the room where Midnight stood. The majestic unicorn peered at me through the glass walls. He lowered his head as if to bow. I turned back to Peter. "I think it was the unicorns," I said with a dumbfounded laugh.

He nodded. My hands found Peter's warm cheeks again. He placed his hands over top of mine and closed his eyes, taking a deep breath. He opened his eyes again and smiled. "You can stop crying," he said. "I'm okay."

I shook my head at the naive request, and my tears continued to pour.

Peter sat up beside me. He brought a hand to my cheek and wiped at my tears. He smiled and put his arms around me, and we held on for a quiet minute. We let go and sat side by side with our feet hanging off the cot.

"Was that you?" asked Peter, glancing over at Razora's lifeless body, grim and ghastly in the water.

I moved a hand to his chest and nodded.

"So you beat her?"

"Yeah," I said with a shrug. "It doesn't feel like I beat anything, though."

Peter put an arm around me, pulling me into him.

"How did you get here, anyway?" I asked, still tight to his side.

"I fell asleep waiting for you on the dock . . . I jumped in right after you."

I shook my head, silently berating myself. "So did you know she was going to go after you?"

"Nah . . . not at first. I kinda figured it out once she started babbling, though." He let go of me and twisted on the bed to meet my eyes. "She sure did underestimate you. You were pretty incredible, Ellie. Where did that all come from?" His eyes were wide with astonishment.

I shrugged as much as I could, but my shoulders were heavy with dreadful guilt. "Yeah, I'm incredible. Incredibly stupid, that is . . . I led you right to her." I scoffed at myself and looked away, tears building in my eyes again.

Peter reached for my hands. "I'm okay, Ellie," he said, squeezing them gently.

I took a deep breath, and my gaze fell to his chest. "Yeah, but . . ." I trailed off, falling into the nightmare memory.

Peter pulled my chin up. He smiled, and it was beautiful. "I'm okay, really." He smiled again, but this time it was sly and mischievous. "I was right, though," he said.

I smiled back now. "I'm sure you were. But what do you mean?"

"Granny Leira's letter . . ." he said, leaning back and pulling it from his pocket. He unfolded the paper. "It had the answer. Look, this whole second part . . . it's about you and this place and about those princess powers of yours." He nudged me playfully. "I think she was trying to tell you you could lend them to someone else."

He pointed at the letter.

Please know it is not a gift, for it has always been yours. It belongs to you, just as it did to me. My soul could not bear to give it to another for fear it would fall into the wrong hands, so it remains yours to do with it what you will. And I worry not, for I know I am leaving it in the palms of someone very special and capable indeed.

I stared at the letter, baffled. "That's quite the riddle. How would I have ever gotten that?"

Peter laughed. "That's how she talked . . . like she was hiding this big secret all the time." He laughed again. "I guess she was." He turned to me. "But maybe she knew you needed to work it out for yourself, ya know? She knew you had it in you."

I pondered that thought and considered my sweet grandmother, so alone and stricken with her struggles. "Poor Granny Leira . . . what a burden this must have all been for her."

Peter looked at me with pained eyes. "Yeah. Sorry, Ellie."

"What are you sorry about?"

"I'm sorry that I didn't really get it before."

I shook my head at him. "No. No way are you going to be apologizing to me right now."

He started to protest.

"No," I repeated with a stern head shake, and tears began to build again.

Peter nodded but leaned into me and whispered quietly, "This wasn't your fault." I shook my head again, but he stopped it with a kiss to my forehead. He put an arm around me and pulled me into him, squeezing me tight. "Why don't we get out of here?"

"That's a really great idea," I said with a nod. I patted his knee and took a steadying breath. "Give me one second. I've got to do one more princessy thing first."

I walked over to where Levvi was kneeling beside Razora. I stared down at her dead body. A sick guilt settled inside me; I was the one who took the life from it.

The blood that oozed darkened beneath her, making her appear just as evil and malicious as ever. It was a dismal sight that sent a mix of uncertainty, sadness, and anger up my spine. I shuddered.

The large merman, Strom, walked over to Razora and pulled her, wet and dripping, from the water.

"I don't know if that was the right thing to do," I said aloud to myself as he carried her out of the room.

Levvi rose to stand beside me and regarded me thoughtfully. "This should never have been your burden, my princess," he said. "I am very sorry for all of your heartache here tonight."

I put my hand on his shoulder, nodding solemnly. "Yeah, it was. Somehow, this was always, exactly, *my* burden." I searched Levvi's eyes. "Can you explain to me why I feel like that?"

Levvi smiled. "You are Glacia's princess." His eyes narrowed lovingly. "And I think you are a very special one at that."

I shook my head and glanced back at Peter. "But I can't be your queen," I said, and I felt the tears in my eyes.

Levvi nodded. "I know. We know," he said, gesturing to the room. "You have helped us tonight and we will forever be grateful." He bowed to me.

"Thank you, Levvi," I said, wiping the tears from my eyes. I looked at him questioningly. "So you really didn't know Leira had given Razora her powers?"

Levvi shook his head. "We knew not. And poor Leira—she must have felt awful about it all. She was a kind soul and would never have done such a thing had she known what Razora was to become."

"No. She didn't know," I agreed, sure in my heart that this was true. I quietly ruminated for a minute. "Do you think I could do it?" I asked. "Give someone my power?"

Levvi thought for a second. "I am not sure. I think the answer to this will lie in you. What do *you* think, my princess?"

I smiled. "I want to try," I said, having already made up my mind. A deep-seated confidence had found its way in, and it was guiding me now—I already knew I could do it.

I screwed my neck around to search for Starla, but my eyes fell on Midnight first.

I walked out of the glass enclosure and over to him. I stared into his big eyes—so blue and peaceful. "Did you and your friends do that?" I asked, gesturing to where Peter was still waiting for me.

Midnight nudged his nose into my shoulder. I wrapped my arms around his strong neck, crying thankful tears. I hugged him tight, then stepped back, brushing my fingers through his soft mane. "Thank you," I whispered with a kiss to his big nose.

I turned to Levvi and Starla, who were standing beside me. I smiled at Starla and reached for her hand. "Come here, Starla," I said. I pulled her with me and we stood together in front of the crowded room.

I looked around at all the faces of those who had gathered. I gazed joyously at each of them. They were happy and free and were without the dark veil of fear to mask their radiant beauty. They each stared back with loving gratitude, and a painful torrent of guilt and heartache came crashing at my soul. I let out a short, sad sigh and spoke to the room.

"I am sorry, but I can't stay," I said. "Leira made a lovely home above. And that is where I belong." I turned to Peter and felt the smile deep inside me.

"However, before I go," I said. "There's something we need to work out."

I turned back to Starla. "Starla," I said, my voice inflated so all could hear. "You and Levvi have shown great strength, loyalty, and, above all else, love—in the *toughest* of circumstances. Through it all, your love has endured. And that love is the key to building this city back up."

I took Starla's other hand and faced her. "Starla, you have the heart of a true princess. It is that unfaltering love that this great city needs." I paused to smile at her. "Starla, I am passing this great duty to you. Will you be so honored as to take the throne here in Glacia?"

A smile beamed across Starla's face. She turned to Levvi, who was smiling back at her.

"Yes," she said happily.

I closed my eyes and held Starla's hands in mine.

I knew what to do. I thought of Glacia and of my love for the beautiful city. I thought of the smiling faces around me, of Levvi and then of Starla, and I let that love grow and pulse through me until I could no longer contain it. With a happy heart, I pushed it from my hands and into Starla's. A slight vibration tickled my palms for a second before stopping.

I opened my eyes and smiled at Starla. She lifted her hands to examine her palms, and together, we saw a faint glow of light lingering on them.

"I think it worked," I said with a laugh.

Starla reached for my hand and turned it over. "Yes," she said. "But I think it is just a small piece of your magic."

I nodded, staring solemnly at the soft glow still on my hands. It was still with me—a part of me—and a strange thought caused me to pause . . . Maybe it always had been.

I smiled up at Starla. "It's enough, though," I said. I reached for Starla, embracing her in a hug. "You're going to make a great queen, Starla."

"I will not let you down, Ellie."

"You couldn't," I said, squeezing her tight.

Levvi was at Starla's side. He put a hand on the small of her back, and she twisted to hug him. He looked at me from over her shoulder. "Thank you, my princess," he said, and he and Starla twirled in a joyous hug.

❧

We stood near the lake above. I held Peter's hand and stared up at the two magical creatures who had somehow become dear friends.

"Will you be there if I ever go back?" I asked Levvi.

"Do you think you will?"

I glanced at Peter and reconsidered. "No . . . probably not."

"Then I will remember you and miss you throughout my days," said Levvi. "It was an honor to have met you." He bowed his head gracefully.

"I'll miss you, too," I said, and tears began to fall.

"Do not fret, dear princess," said Levvi kindly. "You have given us our happy lives back, and my only hope is that you will find the same happiness here and live a long and joyous human life."

"Thank you, Levvi," I said with a smile. I turned to Midnight. "You come visit me anytime." I grinned up at the large beast. He nudged his nose into my shoulder. I reached up, wrapping my arms tightly around him. I held on for a minute, then let go. "Bye," I said to the two magical creatures in front of us.

"Goodbye, Ellie and Peter," said Levvi with a bow. He and Midnight walked back to the water. With a circle of dazzling light, they descended and were out of sight.

I turned to Peter, then back down the beach toward the trails. "Are you ready for this?" I asked.

He followed my gaze hesitantly. "Yeah," he said with a shaky laugh. "What's a little parental wrath after all of that?"

"Yeah," I said. "We've got this." I took his hand and a deep breath, and we started back home together.

32

"One Mississippi. Two Mississippi. Three Mississippi. Four Missi—"

Thunder boomed in the distance, but it was getting closer. I bit at my nails nervously and stared up at the darkening sky. It lit brightly again with another flash, and a loud *clap* rolled ferociously behind it.

"Come on, Peter," I said, looking impatiently toward the alley beside Carle's.

We were supposed to be meeting up at the gazebo after school, but those plans had been locked into place over a week ago, and I hadn't spoken with him since. Neither of us had been clever enough to sort out a backup plan should the weather turn into the fierce and savage beast that currently stalked us.

The pitter-patter of rain sounded on the roof, and another lightning bolt whipped through the sky. This time, the crackle of thunder did not wait for a countdown. On instinct, I bolted out of the gazebo and across the lawn toward Carle's.

It took no time; the clouds poured their buckets, and I was

soaked through and through as I stepped up to the curb on the other side of the street.

I ran at full speed, splashing down the sidewalk with my head low, trying futilely to keep the water off my face. I didn't see Peter as he came running from the side alley and we collided in a wet, blurry mess.

"Peter!" I yelled excitedly over another roll of thunder.

"Come on, let's get inside." He pulled me toward the store.

We pushed open the door, seeking refuge inside. I shook off as much water as I could but would have to resign myself to being a soggy sock for a while. I glanced over at Peter, vainly wiping at his jacket, and saw that we were a matching pair.

"So how did your week in lock-up go?" I asked as I wiped the water from my eyes.

"Eh . . . it wasn't too bad, I guess," he said. "Would have been worse if she knew the truth."

"Yeah," I said with a bleak grin. "You'd be serving life for sure." I took a deep breath and rattled my head, trying to shake off the horrific memories.

I glanced up at Peter. His rain-sodden hair clung to his forehead, and his wet skin glistened in the overhead lights. His cheeks were so rosy, his blinking eyes . . . so beautiful. He was right in front of me, breathing and being perfectly perfect, and my overwhelming joy broke me.

"What's up?" he asked.

I tried to speak, but there was a lump in my throat, blocking my words, so instead, I just cried. I reached up, throwing my arms around him.

He put his arms around me, and my emotions flooded over. My body trembled and waterfalls ran down my face. I didn't care. I would stay like this forever and would never let go.

The door chimed behind us.

"Hey, come here," said Peter, grabbing my hand. He pulled me around the corner to the candy aisle. He took my hands in his, meeting my teary eyes. "It's okay," he said. "I'm okay."

I was still shaking. I took a deep breath to try and stop crying, but it was useless. My breath came out in jagged heaves and there were no levees to hold the tears.

"I . . . thought . . . I . . . lost you . . . and . . ." It was hopeless. My efforts to speak came to an end, and I broke down uncontrollably.

Peter put his arms around me, and I sobbed in them until my eyes ran dry. He waited until I was calm. He then let go and smiled warmly.

"Hey, it looks like the storm has passed," he said, glancing at the store window behind me. "Do you want to go sit outside?"

We sat in the gazebo with the warm sun on our backs, the fresh rain-cleansed air blowing softly around us. I closed my eyes, trying to let the lovely day calm me. I breathed in the beauty with a deep, steadying breath.

"How's your chest?" I asked, glancing fearfully at where the horn had so cruelly pierced him. "Does it still hurt?"

He brought his hand up and rubbed at the spot. "Nah," he said, but his lie was weak.

I narrowed my gaze at him.

He shifted uncomfortably. "Well, just a little sometimes," he said. "But it's getting better."

"Are you sure?"

"Yeah, I don't think it's anything to worry about."

"Okay," I said, but I lingered on his chest, still worried. "You know you can tell your mom if you think it's a problem. You can just say you fell off your bike or something."

"I don't have a bike," said Peter, grinning at me. He saw my unamused scowl. "But yeah, I will. I promise."

"I can't lose you again, Peter." I shook my head at the thought.

"Yeah, I know. You don't have to worry about that. I think those crazy unicorns knew what they were doing. They sure were some miracle workers, huh?"

"Yeah. Thank God," I said, shaking away another horrible thought. "I don't know what I would do without you."

Peter took a heavy breath and sighed. "I think you'd be okay without me."

"God, Peter, don't even say that."

He tilted his head. "Ah . . . I just mean, if I wasn't here . . . in Ocean Lake, you'd be okay." He pressed his lips together and looked at me like he was trying to figure out if that was true.

"That would suck just as much," I said, looking back at him, worried. "Why?"

Peter slumped a little and was slow to answer.

"What?" I asked. He was scaring me.

He sighed and leaned over, resting his elbows on his knees.

I pulled on his forearm to try and get him to sit back up. "Tell me. What is it?"

Peter sat up and turned to me with teary eyes. "We're moving, Ellie."

"What?" I asked because there was no way I had heard that right. He didn't answer me and was quiet again. "Wait, you're not serious, are you?"

He cleared his throat. "Yeah . . . um . . . my mom's going back to school in Portland. My nana lives over there, so . . ." He shrugged and hunched back over his knees.

I stared at his shaggy hair blankly. The dark clouds were back, and they were closing in. "But you can't move," I muttered breathlessly.

Peter's shoulders moved up in an unhelpful shrug.

"Portland?" I breathed. "How far is that?" It would be too far—any distance would be too far. My knees began to shake and my nettlesome tears were back.

Peter moved up and twisted on the bench to face me. He put a hand on my knee to stop me from shaking. "It's not that bad," he said. "Just a few hours away, and I've got to come back a couple of times a month to visit my dad, so . . ." He took a heavy breath and puffed out his cheeks wearily. He exhaled the anxious breath in a slow stream. "But yeah, it sucks."

I paused on Peter's sad eyes. I swayed and took a breath. This wasn't just about me, and I needed to be a friend. I sat up a little straighter and wiped at my eyes, mustering all my will to stop crying. "So . . . what's Portland like?" I asked.

Peter breathed a short, somber sigh. "It's bigger for sure. More people, not so small."

"It sounds like it might be good for you," I said. "You didn't want to be stuck in this dot of a town forever, anyway."

He laughed. "I used to think like that." He smiled at me.

"So what changed your mind, Peter Evans?" I said slyly.

I sighed and bumped his shoulder with mine. "I'm really going to miss you," I said, and any dumb idea I had about not crying was completely abandoned. My eyes poured tears.

Peter turned to me and took my hands in his. A tear dribbled down my cheek and splashed on the backs of our closed hands. "Hey," said Peter, rubbing at the wet drop with his thumb. "It'll be okay. We'll still see each other. We'll visit and stuff, ya know?"

"Yeah." I nodded, but the pesky tears kept falling. "I didn't think of this. I didn't think it was something I had to worry about. I would have been nicer."

"Nicer?" He laughed again. "That wouldn't have been possible."

I tried to smile, but it faltered.

"Hey, don't be sad," said Peter. "Look at me." I looked into his very good eyes. "I'm going to come back to you one day. This is just for now. For now doesn't mean forever, okay?" I shrugged and lowered my head doubtfully. Peter pulled my chin up. "I promise," he said. Then, with a sweet smile, he leaned in and pressed his lips to mine.

"What about this one?" I held up the yellow, moth-eaten T-shirt to Peter.

He was lying on his bed, doing a bad job of pretending to be interested in the task of packing his stuff, the task I had happily assigned myself. They were leaving tomorrow, and his room was still unpacked, and his mom was on him about it, making him stay in until he finished the job—a threat he didn't seem to be too bothered by.

Peter glanced at the shirt. "I don't know, Ellie. I'll just do this later. I'm just going to throw it all in a big bag, anyway. You really don't need to go through all of it."

I frowned at Peter's casual indifference, then turned to the T-shirt in my hands. "Can I have it?"

"You want that T-shirt? It's got a bunch of holes in it."

I put it to my nose. "It smells like you, though . . . and it's soft." I brushed the soft fabric against my cheek.

"Sure," said Peter with a smile. "Do you want my stinky socks, too?" He pushed his feet in the air and waved them at me. "They smell like me."

I threw the T-shirt at him, and he caught it with a smile.

I turned back to the closet and pulled out more shirts. "So you'll be going to school over there?"

"Yeah," huffed Peter. "Mom won't have time to homeschool. It's stupid. I was mostly doing it myself, anyway."

I folded a T-shirt midair and placed it in the box beside me. "I think it'll be good for you."

Peter huffed again. "Why is that?"

"You're going to see, Peter."

"See what?"

"That I'm not the only one."

"What are you talking about?" He looked at me, confused.

"Give me a break, Peter," I said with a smile. "Those girls over there . . . they are going to be swooning. Girls here?" I pointed a finger to my temple and drew circles. "Completely crazy."

He rolled his eyes at me. "We all know you're the crazy one. But if it works out for me." Peter shrugged happily and stretched his arms up behind his head.

"Well, don't be too brooding and cute," I warned. "Because I'm not crazy, and you're going to see that very soon."

Peter rolled off the bed and walked over to me. "Hey, even if you had to worry—which you don't—you wouldn't have to worry."

"Yeah?" I asked hopefully.

"Geez no," he said with pained eyes. "Do you think I'd be that stupid? I really should be fighting with my mom to stay here. It's actually ridiculous how foolish moving away from you is. I'm just still in denial, so it hasn't really hit me yet."

I reached up and gently punched his shoulder. "Then keep your promise," I said. "And come back to me someday."

"You can count on it," he said with a steady nod.

I turned and pulled another shirt from his closet. I was tearing up again and knew I needed this distraction. Peter took the shirt from me and hooked it back onto the rack. "Why don't we get out of here?"

"You've got to pack." I glanced around his messy room.

"I'll get to it later," he said. "It'll take me two minutes. Really."

"Are you sure?"

"Yeah, I don't want to spend my last day with you here packing all my crap." He pushed the ragged T-shirt he was holding into my hand. "And you can have the shirt."

I smiled and brought it to my nose, inhaling deep and long. "Ah," I muttered.

"You know I'm right in front of you, right?"

I lowered the shirt and leaned into Peter, taking in a shaky breath. He smelled better than the shirt—a fresher, full-bodied, and absolutely heartbreaking version of it. I closed my eyes and lingered in the agonizingly knee-melting scent, breaking a little more with every inhale. I opened my eyes and looked at Peter. Yep, I was going to cry. I took another shaky breath to calm myself.

"Hey, you okay?"

I sucked up my tears. "Yeah," I said. "Where do you want to go?"

"Would the lake cheer you up?" he asked with a smile.

I smiled back.

Peter grabbed my hand and my backpack near his door. "Let's go," he said, pulling me out of the room.

"Hey, Mom," said Peter as we headed down the stairs.

Mrs. Evans had made way more progress with her packing than we did. The living room was a warehouse of boxes, and the only thing left in the kitchen was a pizza box and some paper plates and cups. She came around the corner with a crying Liam in her arms. "Mom, we're going to go out for a little while," said Peter.

"Is your room packed?" she asked.

"I'll do it later."

Mrs. Evans looked at Peter, anxious and exhausted. "I'd rather you do it now, Peter."

"Please, Mom. I promise."

She eyed us both with a sigh, looking torn between wanting to be nice and needing to be packed and ready. "All right," she said, giving in. "But not too long. I'm serious, Peter."

"Got it," said Peter, heading toward the door.

We opened the door to a drizzle of rain. Peter held out his palms. He turned to me. "It's not too bad. Do you still want to go?"

"Yeah," I said with a nod.

Something warm and fluffy brushed against my leg. I looked down at the black lab by our feet. I knelt and rubbed her belly. "Let's bring Shadow."

Peter grabbed the umbrella.

"Are you cold?" asked Peter. "I forgot you were wearing shorts."

"No, I'm not cold," I said. I wasn't. I was perfect. We were walking along the edge of the lake. Everything was gray: the sky, the water, the pebbles. Even Shadow running up and down the beach with her misty black coat added to the drab gloominess of the day.

And it all fell in line with my mood, which was perfectly fine with me; a sunny day would have made things so much harder. At least the weather was allowing me to mope.

All the ice was gone from the lake, and the pitter-patter of the rain on the surface of the water was a drone of sweetness to my ears. The water rippled and bubbled with millions of raindrops plunging down into its surface, happily rejoining its liquid family.

The cold, misty air was fresh and smelled new . . . and somehow hopeful. I breathed deep and steady.

We were huddled beneath the umbrella together. Peter bent down to pick up some rocks, and I lowered myself a little when he did. He handed me a stone. "Whoever gets closest to the boulder wins," he said with a smile.

"You're on."

I got out from under the cover of the umbrella. The cool rain on my skin was welcoming. I stood at the edge of the water and tossed my rock through the air, toward the boulder. The small stone was lost in the canvas of gray, but it plunked into the water a second later, landing a few feet short of the boulder. I flopped my shoulders. "Oh God, that was terrible."

Peter laughed and handed me the umbrella. He took his rock and whipped it through the air. I waited for the plunk, but instead, it dinged and bounced off the boulder before falling into the water. I raised my arms and the umbrella to the sky and cheered. "You did it!" I skipped over to him and put my arms around him, bringing the umbrella over us again. "Amazing!"

Peter laughed. "That explains it," he said.

"Explains what?"

"You just easily impress," he said with a smile. "It explains you and me."

The rain started to pick up, and I lowered the umbrella to just above our heads. The pitter-patter sounded loudly on the stretched plastic.

I looked at Peter, my arms still around him. My eyes were full and brimming. "If you only knew," I said, shaking my head at him. I blinked, and the tears pushed down my cheeks. I kept my eyes closed and listened to the pouring rain.

Peter pulled me into a hug. "This sucks," he said.

"Yeah, it sucks," I agreed with a quiet sniff of my nose.

I let go of Peter and handed him the umbrella. I reached behind him for my backpack. He pivoted for me and I unzipped it and pulled out my phone and earbuds.

With a tap on his shoulder, I turned him back around. I attempted to smile but managed only a weak one, and my eyes wouldn't try at all. "We're already crying, so . . ." I placed a bud in my ear and then tucked one into Peter's. I pushed *play* on our song. Holding onto my phone, I reached my arms back up and around Peter, pulling myself as close as I could.

He held me tight, and we swayed to the music, and I cried like a baby the whole time.

34

"I can't believe you're leaving me in this one-horse town all by myself," I said, shaking my head. "You're the only thing it had going for it."

Peter leaned into my ear. "And the mermaids," he whispered.

"Yeah," I said with a quiet smile.

"You're going to stay away from them, right?"

I nodded. "Yeah, I promise."

"You can test out those tail fins in our own lake," he said, gently kicking the side of my shoe. "There's no need to go back down there."

"Yeah, don't worry," I said. "Really, I won't. I've learned my lesson."

"Okay. I just want to make sure." He was eyeing me doubtfully.

"Peter, I should have listened to you the first time. Trust me, I'm not going back."

"Good," he said with a satisfied nod.

We were standing outside by his mom's car. They were getting ready to set off just behind the moving van that had already left.

"Are you about ready, Peter?" his mom called from the porch

as she locked the door. Peter glanced over his shoulder and nodded at her.

"I guess I've gotta go," he said, his voice breaking a little.

I met his tear-filled eyes. "Yeah, okay," I said, my own face a leaky faucet. I sniffed uselessly at my drippy nose.

"Oh, wait," said Peter, using his sleeve to dry his eyes. He opened the car door and pulled something out. "I never got a chance to get you anything." He handed me a rolled-up booklet. "I hope this is okay."

I uncurled it with a happy smile. He had made me a comic book.

On the cover was a young mermaid with a navy-blue tail and blonde hair—with a bright red streak in it just like mine. I flipped through the pages and laughed.

"She's on a quest," said Peter. "For a lost treasure that contains a key that will save her city, and, well . . ." He stopped. "I guess I'll let you read it for yourself."

I closed the book and started to cry again. "I love it." I reached up to hug him, and he put his arms around me and pulled me into a tight hold.

"Okay," I said, moving away. I tilted my head, debating whether or not I should.

Peter looked curious. "What?" he asked.

I smiled at him but swayed in my uncertainty a little more. I sighed and pulled my backpack around in front of me. I unzipped it and pulled out my journal—my new journal, the one I had started since moving to Ocean Lake. I breathed nervously and handed it to Peter.

"What's this?" he asked. He leaned against the car and flipped through it. A smile grew big and wide on his face. "You're giving me your journal?"

I nodded. "I wanted you to know."

He laughed and scanned the pages some more. He held up a pencil drawing I'd done of a drippy, bleeding heart—his name unmistakably written in white script letters in the center. "Wanted me to know what?" he asked with a smirk.

I blushed and brushed up beside him on the car. Peter leaned into me and kissed my forehead, and I closed my eyes and sighed at the sweet touch.

He looked back down at the pages with a laugh. "You're drawing mermaids now?" he asked, pointing at one of a mermaid with a pretty emerald tail. "It's amazing."

The drawing was of Granny Leira, or what I thought Granny Leira as a young mermaid would have looked like. I gave her a bright emerald tail to go with her luxuriously bright red hair.

"Yeah, I hope that's okay. I tore out a few pages of my mermaid babble, though. I just left the drawings. The rest is mostly about you . . . I swear."

"You didn't have to tear them out," said Peter, bumping my shoulder beside him. Peter turned another page. He tilted it to me. "Shouldn't that say Mrs. *Cordelia* Evans?" he asked slyly, pointing at where I'd written the name with just *Ellie*.

I buried my head in my hands. "Oh God, I don't know why I decided to give this to you—so embarrassing."

Peter closed the book. "It's the nicest thing. I don't even know what to say." He pushed off the car and turned to face me. "You really are like a dream . . ." His eyes fell to his feet. "And this is the part where I have to wake up, I guess," he said, shuffling them on the dirty pavement.

"Don't wake up," I said. "You don't have to."

Peter leaned into me and put his arms around me. "Thank you, Ellie," he said. "For everything."

I shook my head against his shoulder. "Stop thanking me like you're never going to see me again," I said. "This is not goodbye, okay?"

"Okay. No goodbyes. That's easier."

We held on for another short minute. Then Peter squeezed me tight one last time before letting me go. He quietly stared at me with a sad smile on his face. He reluctantly tilted his head toward the car door and opened it. "I'll see you later, Cordelia."

"See you later, Peter," I said with a breaking heart.

He got in the car with his mom and Liam. They were buckled and ready, and the car was rolling away before I was.

I waved at Peter as they drove off, and then he was gone.

35

I lay in my bed, gazing at the stars through my skylight. I smiled as a shooting star flashed by. I closed my eyes and made a wish. My wish was that Peter would come back. I sighed, knowing it wasn't going to happen. He had already been gone a week, and I was already missing him.

I turned over in my bed. I stared across my room at the small cabinet near the top of the stairs. I got up and walked over to it. I opened the door and pulled on the light.

I stared at the stack of shoeboxes inside. This was where I had found my locket. It was safely back in Dad's office now. I had finally gotten the chance to return it this afternoon, and I sure was relieved to have that weight off me.

I picked up one of the shoeboxes and rummaged through it. More photos. I smiled brightly as I went through them. I was delighted to see they were pictures of Midnight and some of the other unicorns whom I had never met.

"Oh my god," I said, putting my hand to my smiling lips. It was Levvi and Starla sitting together on the porch just outside. From the looks of it, all the pictures had been taken outside in my own backyard. I laughed at the thought.

"How have I never seen these?" I wondered aloud. Then a thought came to me. I quickly picked up the same box I had opened the night we first moved in, the one that had the photos of Granny Leira mixed with the bright, blurry ones. It came as no surprise that all the bright, overexposed photos that had been in this very box were now perfectly developed pictures of my unicorn and mermaid friends. And Granny Leira was with them, too.

These must have been taken toward the end. She was older in them, but she had the same warm smile I'd seen on her before, when she posed with her husband and children in the aged photos from long ago.

I picked up the photos one by one to look at them until I had a stack in my hands. I started to place them back in the empty box when I noticed the paper that lined the bottom had a slight bulge in it. I pulled back the liner in order to release the photos that I was sure had gotten stuck there, but instead, I found a folded piece of notepaper.

I put the photos down and opened the paper. It was a letter, and it was addressed to *me*. I read it quietly, then sat pensive and peaceful and smiling with the letter in my hand.

I was jolted out of my reverie when my phone rang. I hurried over and grabbed it from under my pillow.

"Hello," I said eagerly.

"Hey, Ellie. It's Peter."

I fell on my back and floated away in a puffy white cloud.

"Hey, Peter," I said with a smile.

"Sorry I haven't called sooner. We know nothing about setting up phones. Me, my mom, and Nanna—none of us. You'd think we'd come out of an eighties sitcom the way we struggled. It was pathetic."

I laughed. "You should have given it to me before you left."

"Yeah, I should've. I actually had it, too."

"So this is your phone? Just yours?"

"Yeah," he said.

"Good. It's about time your Mom gives into the future."

"Yeah, well, I told her I was going to stay there with my dad if she didn't get me one."

"Was that an option?" I asked, somewhat hopeful.

"No. Not really. He doesn't have custody. Maybe someday, though."

"Yeah, maybe," I said but thought better of it. "But I think you're probably better off with your mom, right?"

"Yeah," agreed Peter.

The line was quiet.

"So how do you like it over there?" I asked.

"Ah, it's all right. I mean, it's kinda cool, I guess. I think you'd like it. It's more like a city . . . There's museums and coffee shops and stuff. Probably nothing like New York, but it feels a whole lot bigger than Ocean Lake did."

"That sounds great," I said with a breathy laugh that was a mix of a little happy for him and a little sad for both of us.

My next breath came in shaky. "I can't wait to visit. This place has gotten even smaller since you left . . . if you can believe that."

Peter was quiet on the other end for a second. He sighed. "I miss you, too."

My eyes began to water. I wiped at the tears and cleared my throat. "Hey, can I read you something I just found in my closet?"

"Sure, I guess," said Peter.

"It's a letter from Granny Leira."

"Oh, okay," he said, suddenly understanding.

I read the letter.

Dearest Cordelia,

I have hidden this letter here in hopes that you will find it one day. I do not think you will mind that I wanted to keep the contents herein just between you and me. As a result, it will remain hidden until it is found by you, whenever that may be. I will trust that the curious child that you are will find it before it has been too long.

I do hope that you like your new home here. I think that you will find that this is truly your home in more ways than you ever realized. I wanted to bring you here because I thought it was only fair that you had all the pieces and knew all the secrets that make you who you truly are. If right now this does not make sense, do not worry—it will in time.

I wanted to do for you what I could not do for your mother, which is to give you the choice to live your life the way you want to live it.

In the past, I made the mistake of taking that decision away from her. When my son Matthew had a daughter, I had already scared him enough with my stories that, sadly, he thought hiding her was his only option.

I have regretted this throughout all of my days, and I am sorry that I have missed her life and yours. I know I do not deserve your forgiveness. Just please understand, I have always loved you and your mother and have always only wanted the best for you both.

Even now the decision to bring you here is a difficult one for me. Sometimes, even when you're quite old, it's hard to know what the right thing to do is. But I have confidence that a princess can choose her own path, just as I chose mine.

Remember to trust your heart, for it is your most honest guide and a princess's heart will never lead her astray.

I love you, Cordelia.

Your loving,
Granny Leira

P.S. I have a friend named Peter here whom I think you might get along with. He lives across town but plays back at the lake often. Tell him I sent you and tell him thank you for keeping a dear old lady company.

I lowered the paper.

"That's the Granny Leira I remember," said Peter.

"She liked you a lot," I said. "Somehow she knew we were going to find each other."

"We almost missed each other, though."

"How do you mean?"

"Well, you only just moved there a few months ago. Any later and I would have been gone already. We wouldn't have met."

I shook my head against my pillow. "That never would have happened," I said.

"Oh, no?"

"Nope. Peter, I was always going to find you."

"Is that right?" he asked. I heard the smile in his voice.

"Yeah," I said, smiling back.

"So you think *you* found *me*?"

"Yeah, I found you. You were the piece I was searching for all along. Don't you know? So I could start my story."

"You got quite the unexpected story, didn't you?"

"Yeah, I guess I did. It kind of swept me up. And you know what, Peter Evans?"

"What?"

"You were the best part."

Peter laughed. "So, Cordelia, are you ready for the next chapter?"

I smiled. "I am . . . as long as it includes you."

Epilogue

I stood on the dock, breathing in the fresh night air. The warm summer breeze soothed and comforted as it brushed across my skin.

I closed my eyes and listened to the harmonious drone of a million crickets and the soft lapping of the waves as they hit the wooden posts below me.

The tranquil waters glittered under the moonlight, calling to my heart. I took a blissful breath. There was no point in trying to resist it anymore—I wouldn't be able to.

I stepped on the backs of my shoes to remove them, then pulled off Peter's hoodie and threw it on top.

I smiled down at the water. "Okay," I said, "it's just you and me now."

And with one more breath, I jumped in.

Thank you so much for reading Ellie and Peter's story.
I hope you enjoyed it as much as I enjoyed writing it! Their story continues in *Lights at Midnight* Book 2: *Shadows of Stars*

Get *Shadows of Stars* on Amazon today!
https://www.amazon.com/dp/B091J4RLT5

Join my mailing list for news and updates:
https://www.orchidleigh.com/viplist

ABOUT THE AUTHOR

Orchid Leigh lives in Maine with her husband and two children.

She loves music, movies, painting, and listening to the rain. When she isn't writing, she can usually be found playing video games with her kids, dabbling with her paints, or singing karaoke to herself.

Lights at Midnight is her first novel.

Want to keep up with Orchid's enchanting stories?
Follow her online at:
Website: orchidleigh.com
Instagram: @orchidleigh

Printed in Great Britain
by Amazon